Grimm

CONTROVERSIAL CATTLE QUEEN

Susie Bowman was quite ... small ranchers are ... was almost a leg ... ugh, beautiful, fre ... out her ranching.

To the local ju ... sie was just "a very eccentric woman who flaunts the laws of God and man." And he was gonna hound her until he brought her to "justice."

To Bob Norberg, who rode up from Denver to lend her a hand, Susie was the most damnably fascinating woman who ever forked a horse.

And to the ruthless killer hired to gun her down, Susie made a beautiful target.

Bantam Books by Wayne D. Overholser

THE CATTLE QUEEN FEUD
WAR IN SANDOVAL COUNTY

THE
CATTLE
QUEEN
FEUD

Wayne D. Overholser

BANTAM BOOKS · TORONTO · NEW YORK · LONDON

THE CATTLE QUEEN FEUD
A Bantam Book / July 1979

ISBN 0-553-13043-9

Published simultaneously in the United States and Canada

Bantam Books are published by Bantam Books, Inc. Its trademark,
consisting of the words "Bantam Books" and the portrayal of a
bantam, is Registered in U.S. Patent and Trademark Office and in
other countries. Marca Registrada. Bantam Books, Inc., 666 Fifth
Avenue, New York, New York 10019

THE
CATTLE
QUEEN
FEUD

Chapter I

When Sid Gorman sent an office boy to tell me I was wanted in his office, I was annoyed, to make an understatement. I had spent a week running down a story about corruption in the police department and I hadn't finished writing it when I got the word. I hesitated, then got up and headed for the big man's office. When Sid Gorman spoke, no one argued.

I'd worked for the *Denver Daily Chronicle* for fifteen years. I was thirty now and I'd been getting ink under my fingernails for what seemed a long time. Sid hired me when I was a kid. He'd been running the *Chronicle* for a long time before that and he was getting old. Calling him old meant that he was grumpy and short-tempered and sharp-tongued, and all the other synonyms that added up to being hard to get along with. But he had seen something of promise in a green country kid, and I had always been grateful.

Sid was sitting at his desk with his head down, the usual green eyeshade pulled down over his forehead, the inevitable cigarette hanging out of one corner of his mouth. He looked up when he heard the door shut, threw his pencil down, and leaned back.

He swore, banged his fist against the desktop, and muttered, "Damned cub reporters can't spell anymore. I remember you could. The world's going to hell in a hand basket when I have to correct spelling mistakes in words like 'euphoria'."

He grinned, figuring that a compliment would make me

1

feel good. It should, there having been so few of them over the years. His grins were few and far between, too. He was a tough old bird, a tyrant if there ever was one, but he was the best newspaperman I knew. Still, I had a feeling about this I didn't like. He was setting me up for a job I wouldn't want to take.

"Yes, sir," I said. "I guess spelling wasn't one of my problems."

"Sit down, Bob," he said. "Where did you get this 'sir' business? I'm still Sid around here."

I sat down and didn't say anything. The chair across from his desk was straightbacked and hard-bottomed, the most uncomfortable chair I had ever sat in. I think he'd had it made that way so no one would take any more of his time than necessary.

"I'm going to send you on an assignment that will take some time," he said. "It will be dangerous and challenging and will give you an unlimited expense account. Well, almost."

I knew what that meant, too. He was promising to be generous, a carrot-on-a-stick maneuver, but I'd sure as hell better be ready to account for every cent I spent when I got back.

"Sounds good," I said, and let it go at that.

"It is," he said. "What's more, it will carry the Bob Norberg byline and make you rich and famous."

He leaned back and watched me for a moment. For the first time I had the feeling he was uncertain, a feeling he seldom had. He was afraid I'd turn him down, which probably meant I'd be fired if I did. I knew he didn't want to do that, so he was building the job up for all he was worth.

"That's what I've always wanted to be," I said. "Rich and famous."

"I would guess that after you've wired the story in to us, you'll come back and write a book about the whole business." He hesitated, then added, "I believe you were raised on a ranch and during vacations went back home to help your dad."

"Up until a couple of years ago when he sold out to Ike Kirby," I said. "He died last year."

"Ike Kirby," he said, knowing the name had particular meaning to me.

He'd worked me into a corner. I knew damned well he was aware of the feeling I had for Ike Kirby, who was a big Wyoming cowman, one of the old arrogant kind who didn't know we were out of the eighteenth century. He made his own laws, and if a

2

lawman in his area didn't suit him, he had means of getting rid of him.

Kirby had steadily gobbled up the ranches around my old home in southern Wyoming until ours had been the only one left. When Dad wouldn't sell, Kirby closed him off so he couldn't move his beef to the shipping pens in Cheyenne. Against the law, sure, but who was going to buck Ike Kirby?

Dad finally sold out to Kirby because he didn't have any choice. He left the state, but soon died. Kirby killed him as surely as if he had put a bullet through his heart. I had told myself that if I ever had a chance to get Ike Kirby, I'd do it. From the way Gorman was looking at me right then, I could guess I was going to have my chance.

Gorman hadn't been afraid I'd turn the job down. He'd just been playing cat and mouse with me. He'd done it before, a game that gave him a perverse kind of pleasure. It always made me mad, but I didn't show it.

"It's a familiar name," I said, and then shut my mouth until he made the deal clear.

"Well, now," he said, "this job is going to be a vacation for you. You'll enjoy it and you'll be doing the *Chronicle* a favor. It'll increase our circulation." He jabbed a forefinger at me. "You're going to Canby and you're going to put a knife into that old bastard's heart. Or a bullet. Do you have a gun?"

"Yes," I said, "and I can use it, but I don't see the connection between Kirby and Canby. I'm not familiar with that corner of the state."

"You will be," he said. "The connection is that Kirby is crucifying Susie Bowman. You've heard of her."

I nodded. I'd heard of her, but that was about all. She had been tried for rustling and the trial had ended in a hung jury. She was to be tried again late that summer, but things like that happen all the time in western states. Not with women maybe, but I couldn't see that her being a woman made her case that important.

"I've never met the woman," Gorman went on, "but it makes me mad as hell for a man like Kirby, who throws his weight around, to ruin a woman. I think the public will want to read about it. We always root for the underdog and that's Susie Bowman. The way things stack up now, I'd say she's headed for the Canon City pen."

He stopped to reach for a cigarette. "Susie Bowman is the

3

heroine of your story. Kirby is the villain. But there are a bunch of subvillains and subheroes that you'll meet. One of the subvillains is Judge Oscar Wirt. He tried her before and he'll try her again, and he's bound to convict her. The sheriff is worse. Kirby has him in his hip pocket. I want you to talk to both of them. Tell them why you're there. I told you it's a dangerous job. Somebody will try to kill you. No doubt about it."

"Just exactly what do you want?" I demanded. "It strikes me that I'm a lamb being led to the slaughter."

He nodded grimly. "In all honesty I have to admit that might be the case. I want you to know that before you start."

I wasn't going to back out, now that I knew Ike Kirby was involved. Still, this wasn't the way Sid Gorman usually went at a thing like this, and it bothered me. I said, "I'm still in the dark. What's Susie Bowman's part in all of this? I mean, what makes her so interesting to you?"

"She's an extraordinary woman," he said. "Actually she's the leader of the small ranchers who live in Smith's Cove, a symbol of their resistance to Kirby who is trying to take over the Cove. It would be a perfect spot for him to winter a herd before he drives north to the railroad at Rawlins. I don't think she's guilty of rustling. I think Kirby framed her, and with Judge Wirt hearing the case, she'll be convicted unless something is done for her."

"You expect me to do that something?" I demanded.

He nodded. "You have never been one to deny the power of the press. I'm proud to say that the *Chronicle* has considerable weight all over the Rocky Mountain region. Now as to what I want. Do you still have your work clothes you wore when you helped your father?"

"Yes, but I don't see..."

"Wear them," he said tersely. "They'll laugh you out of Canby if you go over there wearing city duds."

"I'll look like a saddle bum," I objected.

"Good," he said. "It will endear you to their hearts. Canby is a cow town, so there'll be plenty of saddle bums around."

He lit his cigarette, then sat there staring at me, waiting, I guessed, to see what I would do or say. After about half a minute, I burst out, "Well, by God, Sid, I never knew you to beat the devil around the bush the way you're doing today. I've got to know exactly what you want me to do."

"First, I want you to talk to Judge Wirt, then the sheriff,

4

and finally a cowboy named Chip Malone if you can find him."
Gorman answered. "He used to work for Susie and her sister
Janey. He can tell you more about them and the situation than
anybody else—if he'll talk, and I see no reason why he wouldn't.
Then I want you to rent or buy a horse and ride out to Smith
Cove. Get a job with Susie or anybody else you can catch on
with. Stay there as long as you need to. I want to know anything
you turn up that's pertinent."

So he wanted me to go back to cowboying. I could do it,
all right, and in a situation like this it might be interesting. I
guess I was a little bored, sitting here in Denver for months and
not getting out on a ranch the way I had when my father was
alive, but Gorman didn't know that. Maybe this was the reason
he had been hesitant about getting down to cases, thinking I
wouldn't want to go back to being a cowboy.

I rose, still a little uneasy about the whole affair. I said,
"I'll catch the train in the morning."

He sat there like a miniature, wrinkled-up little Buddha,
staring at me through the smoke that drifted up from his
cigarette. I reached the door, then stopped as he said, "One more
thing, Bob. I didn't know whether to tell you this or not, since it
may have nothing to do with Smith's Cove or Susie or your
assignment, but I guess you'd better know.

"About a week ago Kirby came down from Wyoming,
and Judge Wirt and a third man came in from Canby. They met
in a Denver hotel room with a known assassin named Van
Tatum, who has been hanging around town for a month or
more. I don't know what they talked about, but I do know
Tatum left town two days later."

I considered the ramifications of this tidbit. I figured Sid
thought it had something to do with my assignment or he
wouldn't have mentioned it. I said, "I'll be on the lookout for
him. How did you find out about this meeting?"

"I've got spies out everywhere," he said, as he rose and
crossed the office to where I stood by the door. He held his hand
out and I shook it. "Good luck, Bob."

"I may need it," I said, and left the room.

My story about police corruption would have to wait, but
as I walked to my desk a new thought came to me that sent a little
prickle of fear down my spine. He had never shaken hands with
me before, when he'd sent me on an assignment. I had a distinct
feeling that he never expected to see me alive again.

Chapter II

I arrived in Canby early Sunday morning, bleary-eyed and tired because I hadn't slept much during the long ride from Denver. There were no Pullmans on the train, so it was a matter of leaning back in my coach seat and closing my eyes and hoping to sleep. A woman in the other end of the car had a sick baby who cried most of the night. I suppose I did sleep a few minutes at a time, but it wasn't enough to help.

I carried my suitcase two blocks to the Canby Hotel, took a room, and shaved and washed up. I felt better then, and I felt still better after I had gone downstairs to the dining room and had a breakfast of ham and eggs and three cups of coffee.

As I paid for my breakfast, I asked the clerk how people dressed in Canby when they went to church. He looked me over, from my sweat-stained Stetson to my boots with the run-over heels, and shook his head as if puzzled. It didn't add up, my cowboy duds on the one hand, and my pale face on the other. Every working cowboy I had ever seen had a face as dark as tanned leather.

6

"About like you," he said. "In winter some of the businessmen wear suits and ties and white shirts, but it's pretty hot now to dress up."

"What's the nearest church?" I asked.

"The Methodist is a block north," he answered.

"When does the morning service start?"

"Eleven."

I glanced at the pendulum clock above the desk. It was ten minutes before eleven. I said, "Thank you," and walked out into the sunlight, leaving the clerk staring at my back as puzzled as ever.

The Methodist church was similar to the church I had gone to in southern Wyoming when I'd been home. It would seat about one hundred people, I estimated, and was half full when the service started. A chart on the wall behind the preacher announced that the Sunday School attendance had been 52 and the collection had been $9.46. It also gave the numbers of songs we were to sing that morning, and we started with "The Church in the Wildwood" a minute or so after I sat down. The pianist was a cute blonde in her early twenties, and I wondered how I was going to work it so I could meet her.

I guess I didn't listen to the sermon very attentively. The blonde had left the piano and sat down in a front pew, so all I could see was the back of her head. I got to thinking about my reason for being in Canby, and why Sid Gorman had thought enough of Susie Bowman's problem to send me kiting off up here two hundred miles from Denver.

I knew there weren't many cases like Susie's these days, because law and order had come to most of the cattle country, and there weren't many cowmen like Ike Kirby any more. But I was haunted by a notion I couldn't get out of my head, that Sid had more of a motive in sending me up here than he'd told me. Any newsman is supposed to be impartial and objective, but he sure as hell wasn't impartial or objective about this one. He was on Susie's side all the way.

The next thing I knew we were standing and singing the final hymn, then a prayer, and people began filing out. Several came to me and shook hands and hoped I would return. I'm sure I looked out of place. They could tell as well as the hotel clerk had that I wasn't a working cowboy, but no one asked me where I had come from or why I was there, and I appreciated that. I just hadn't thought up a good lie to tell them.

7

As I shook hands with the preacher, I asked, "Are you free any time today? I'd like to have a talk with you."

He was short and round-faced, a little on the plump side, having fed too well on fried chicken and meat loaf at church suppers. But he seemed a kindly man, although he obviously was as puzzled about me as the others.

"My wife and I have been invited to dinner by one of our church families," he said, "but we should be finished by four o'clock. I'll be in my office then. It's on the other side of the building. The front door will be locked, so if you will come around to the rear, you'll see the door that opens into the office, Mr...."

"Norberg," I said. "Bob Norberg. I'll be there."

"Fine," he said. "I'm John Ross. I'm glad you were able to attend the service this morning."

"I enjoyed it," I lied, and turned away to let the line move forward so others could shake hands with him.

Outside I clapped my Stetson on my head and waited a minute or two to see if the blonde pianist would come out, but she didn't, so I walked away. I spent an hour or more exploring the town. It was little different from other cow towns I knew except that it seemed less touched by time and progress than most. None of the streets were paved. The courthouse was a frame building that probably dated back to the first year that Tremont County had been organized. It needed painting and the lawn had more dandelions than grass, but that was more or less normal.

Main Street looked prosperous. I counted three general stores, one other hotel in addition to the one where I was staying, a couple of livery stables, one blacksmith shop, two banks, four saloons, and a saddle and harness shop. There were also a number of smaller shops and offices.

The railroad had reached Canby only a couple of years before, and if I remembered right, the town had doubled in population in that time. The talk was that James Tremont, one of Colorado's railroad moguls, had pushed the rails to Canby and intended to go on to Salt Lake City. This rumor had been responsible for the spurt of growth the town had made, but Tremont had not been able to raise the capital he needed, so he was stymied for the time being. It was my guess that Canby would probably remain the end of steel.

There was one block of homes north of the business

section that belonged to the wealthy citizens of Canby: the bankers, the doctors, the undertaker, and perhaps the merchants. One of them probably belonged to Judge Oscar Wirt. I walked along the boardwalk slowly trying to guess which one. They were somewhat similar with their mansard roofs, iron fences, carefully kept lawns, porch swings, and colored glass in their front doors. I gave up trying to guess which one belonged to the Judge. I wondered if I would find out before I left town.

Returning to the hotel, I ate dinner, then asked the clerk if he knew Chip Malone. He nodded, still looking at me with that quizzical expression as if he just couldn't place me in the right pigeonhole.

"Sure, everybody knows Chip," he said. "You'll find him in the Red Front Livery Stable. He's been working there all winter. The last I heard he hadn't found a summer job riding for any of the big outfits."

I thanked him and stepped into the street, wondering why everybody would know Chip Malone. I remembered seeing the stable one block east. A moment later I stepped through the archway but I didn't see anybody. Then I noticed the open door of the tack room. A young man was sitting at a dust-covered desk, slouched down with his chin on his chest. He was sound asleep.

I stopped in the doorway, not wanting to wake him, but there didn't seem to be anyone else around. I cleared my throat, and the young man jumped, his head jerking up. He stared at me as one hand moved toward the top drawer of the desk.

"I'm looking for Chip Malone," I said.

"You found him," he said, the hand opening the drawer and moving inside.

He was holding the butt of a gun, I thought, and that didn't make sense. He froze, his gaze still on me. I couldn't see the hand, but I was sure he'd lifted the gun from the drawer and was waiting for me to make my business known. As far as I had been able to tell from walking around the town, it was peaceful enough, so I didn't see any reason for him to be so jumpy.

"I'd like to talk to you," I said. "I just got into town this morning. I'm Bob Norberg from the *Denver Daily Chronicle*. I'm looking into the Susie Bowman case."

He stood up, slamming the drawer shut. He still didn't say anything, his gaze moving from my head to my toes and back again. He had deep crow's feet around his eyes that had been cut

9

there by sun and wind—a typical cowboy, I thought, slim and long-legged. He was good-looking, with a square jaw and a full-lipped mouth. He chewed on his lower lip a moment, his dark eyes wary.

"I'm not armed," I said, holding one of my cards out to him, "and I'm not here to threaten you. If I had wanted to harm you, I'd have done it when you were sleeping."

"Yeah, reckon you would," he said as he took the card. He studied it a moment, then moved toward me and held out his hand. "I'm a mite skittish. You never know about strangers. I don't like the smell of things in this town one damned bit. We're sitting on a powder keg. The fuse is lit and it's just about long enough to reach from here to the day of Susie's trial."

I liked his handshake, a good, firm grip with none of the lukewarm slackness and deadfish feeling that characterize some men. I'm afraid of that kind of handshake. It's not always a hint of instability or meanness or untrustworthiness, but it has seemed to me that over the years it's been a pretty good indication of what's in a man.

"I thought Susie's trial wasn't coming for a couple of months," I said, "so I didn't think there would be any trouble now."

"There's always trouble when a man like Ike Kirby can thumb his nose at the law and get away with it." He motioned to a cane-bottomed chair with a broken back that was set against the opposite wall. "Sit down. What do you want to know about Susie that I can tell you?"

I didn't sit down because I sensed this wasn't the time to press him. I said, "I'm not familiar with the evidence that was brought up in the trial. I was given this assignment and told to catch the next train to Canby, but as I remember it, you were the key witness."

"That's right, and it's the reason I'm so damned boogery. If I get plugged before the trial, Susie will go to the pen as sure as hell's hot."

"Why wasn't she acquitted in the first trial?" I asked. "Or is she guilty?"

"Hell, no, she's not guilty," he snapped. "Now I ain't saying that Susie never had no slow elk for supper. Everybody in the Cove has and a man like Kirby can afford to lose a few head, but he don't think so. I was working for Susie at the time they

10

arrested her and I know she hadn't killed and butchered the heifer that the hide they found on the fence had come from."

"Then why wasn't she...?"

"Because a couple of Goddamned jurors were bought off," he interrupted. "I can't prove it, but it's the only way it makes any sense. With Judge Wirt giving instructions to the jury, it was a pat hand."

"Can I quote you on that?"

"Sure," he said. "Won't hurt nothing because everybody knows where I stand. Just remember I said I couldn't prove it."

He moved past me and went on out through the archway and put his back to the front wall of the stable. He reached for tobacco and paper and rolled a smoke. I followed him, knowing there was a lot more he could tell me, but it could wait.

"I guess you're thinking that any man can print a card and claim he's working for the *Chronicle*."

"Keerect." He nodded as he sealed his cigarette and lighted it. "If you're bucking the kind of power that a man like Kirby has, you take a good, long second look before you trust anybody. I'll tell you something else, too, if you're on the level. When Kirby and some of the rest of 'em find out who you are and what you're doing, they'll kill you just like they're fixing to kill me. I don't know how they aim to do it, but you can bet your bottom dollar they're gonna try."

"Why will they try to kill me?" I asked.

"Because they don't want any more publicity than they've already got," he answered. "A paper like the *Chronicle* sways the way a lot of people think. The less said about Susie's case, the better."

"I'm not going to fool around with them," I said. "I aim to see Wirt and the sheriff tomorrow."

"Don't bother with the sheriff," Malone said. "He ain't worth a damn. He's just a fat lackey who does what Kirby says. He was bought and paid for the day he was elected, which was by the help of the votes of some men who've been dead for five years."

I hadn't heard that before and it was worth following up, but when I glanced at my watch, I saw I didn't have time then. It was almost four. I said, "I've got to go. I want to talk to you again. I'll buy you a drink if I can catch you when you're not working."

"I'll be around if I ain't dead." As I turned away, he added. "One more thing. If you are really a reporter, how are you going to write this story? Against Susie or for her?"

I paused, not sure how to answer. I knew that if what I dug up indicated Susie was guilty, Sid Gorman would call me back or change what I'd written so it sounded as if I was saying something I wasn't. I'd seen him do it more than once. In my opinion this was the one fault that kept him from being recognized as the outstanding newspaperman west of the Mississippi. He simply could not keep his feelings out of any subject he felt strongly about, and he certainly felt strongly about Susie Bowman.

"A newspaper is supposed to be impartial," I said, and walked away.

Chapter III

The Reverend John Ross was sitting at his desk, the door of his office open. When he saw me, he said, "Come in, Mr. Norberg. You're right on time."

I stepped into his office, saying, "I hope I'm not inconveniencing you."

"Not at all." He motioned me to a chair. "Sit down. I'll close the door if this is something you consider private. Otherwise I'll leave it open. It's a warm day for early June."

I sat down, suddenly uneasy for some reason that I could not pinpoint. I sensed that the preacher was nervous and I wondered about that. It was in the overly pink color of his cheeks, the slight tremor of his hands as he placed them palm down on the desk in front of him.

"No, leave it open." I drew a long breath as I sat down and decided to plunge in head first. "Do you know Susie Bowman?"

He swallowed, his gaze dropping to the desktop. "Yes, I know her. That is, I know her by sight. She never comes to church and Smith Cove is a long ways from town, so I never ride out there unless they call me for a funeral or a wedding, and that doesn't happen very often."

"Do you consider her guilty of rustling?"

He looked up, acting as if the question shocked him. "Why, that is a strange question, Mr. Norberg. I have no way of knowing, since the first trial resulted in a hung jury. I can tell you that Judge Wirt believes she is guilty and that a great injustice was done when she was not convicted in the first trial. In other words, he is irritated that they have to go through another trial, which he considers unnecessary and an added expense that the county should not have to pay for." He looked straight at me then and asked, "Why?"

I handed him my card. "I know I don't look like a reporter on a city newspaper, but my boss thought I would be less conspicuous if I dressed this way. I'm here to do a story on Susie, and I expect to ride out to the Cove in a day or so and meet her. I understand she is a sort of character."

He stared at the card, then at me, and at the card again. He said, "This is extraordinary, Mr. Norberg. You see, my wife and I had dinner with Judge Wirt and his family today. He is one of the stalwarts in our church and, as you may know, one of the pillars of the community. He is upset about the Susie Bowman business because she is a troublemaker who has lived by her standards all of her life and continues to do so, regardless of the law of the land. This behavior worries the Judge because the people who live in the Cove respect and look up to her."

"You would say she's a community leader?"

"Oddly enough, she is," Ross agreed. "When you learn more about her, you'll wonder why. She's an amoral woman who defies all of the moral standards which have made our country great, so why the people who live in the Cove respect her is more than I can understand."

He made a gesture as if to dismiss the subject of Susie Bowman. "The extraordinary aspect of your visit to me is that Judge Wirt was mentioning at dinner that he expected a Denver reporter to show up in Canby, and you turn out to be the very man he was expecting."

This floored me. I had no idea how Judge Wirt or anybody else in Canby would know that Sid Gorman was planning to send me here. I shook my head. "I don't know why he expected me."

"I can't tell you that." Ross rose as if terminating the interview. "I have only one thing to say to you, Mr. Norberg. I will repeat what the Judge said to me at dinner. We do not appreciate a Denver newspaper meddling in our affairs. We have a local newspaper. We depend on it to disseminate the news that concerns our county. You are not welcome here. You are not safe. For your sake, I urge you to take the morning train back to Denver."

I rose, too, anger stirring in me. "Is this a threat?"

"Not at all. I'm concerned about your safety."

"Do you know Ike Kirby?"

"Why?"

"I have a theory that he's the one who wants me to leave Canby, and wants whatever publicity the Susie Bowman case has to come through the local newspaper."

He took a handkerchief from his pocket and wiped his face. He said, "I don't know what Mr. Kirby wants. I believe that's all we have to say to each other. Good day, sir."

There was nothing for me to do but say good day and leave his office. As I walked slowly toward Main Street, it struck me that John Ross might be perfectly honest in his attitude about Susie Bowman and my presence in Tremont County, but again he might simply be parroting the Kirby-Wirt line of thinking—that he was bought and paid for just as Wirt apparently was.

When I reached the corner before making the turn to Main Street, I glanced back and saw the Reverend John Ross leave his office and hurry down the street toward the block of prosperous-looking houses I had seen earlier that day. He wasn't wasting any time before reporting to Judge Wirt.

Main Street had been practically deserted all day. I walked along it again, looking at the store windows but really not seeing what was in them. I considered discarding Gorman's instructions to see Judge Wirt and the sheriff, to rent a horse in the morning and ride out to the Cove. I needed to see and talk to Susie Bowman.

No, it wouldn't do. For one thing, it never paid to ignore Gorman's orders. That was one of the first things I had learned when I went to work for the *Chronicle*. Gorman always seemed to know when I hadn't carried out his orders. I'd get a tongue-lashing for disobeying and a fine to boot. He was a dictator, and I'd made up my mind to live with it as long as I worked for the *Chronicle*.

Another point was the undisputed fact that I needed to learn more about the background of the case than I knew now, and I had to get it in town. Anything I learned from Susie Bowman and her friends in the Cove would be biased, to say the least. Even pumping Chip Malone as I intended to do tomorrow would not be enough.

I'd go to the newspaper office and look over the back issues for the last five years. If the editor was a Kirby man, I'd be in trouble. I'd soon find out about that. The other possibility was the courthouse, but I'd never had much luck working with legal documents. Besides, the county officials were probably Kirby hirelings and would likely refuse to let me see the pertinent papers.

I returned to the hotel, knowing I'd have to play the game according to plan. I ate supper, then went upstairs to my room and spent an hour writing my first dispatch for the *Chronicle*. I didn't have anything earthshaking to say, but I built up the point that I had been warned to leave town. The preacher's suggestion certainly had been a veiled threat.

There were people and interests in Canby and Tremont County that wanted to hide their actions and therefore objected to publicity. I said that only those who were afraid of the light wanted to stay in the dark. I did not mention any names. That would come later.

I folded the sheets of paper, slipped them into an envelope, and stamped and sealed it. I went back down to the street, remembering that the post office was in the next block beside the First National Bank. I mailed the letter and walked slowly back through the gathering twilight along the deserted street, thinking that it bore little resemblance to the Canby I'd see if I were here on a Saturday night, especially at shipping time.

Still, as quiet as it was, I felt a chill travel down my spine. I had always been afraid of men who had an extreme fear of publicity. As I thought back over my talk with the Reverend John Ross, and his inordinate haste to inform someone of my visit probably Judge Wirt, the future began to loom more ominous than ever. The question was how far men would go to prevent the publicity they feared. If it was a bluff, I had nothing to fear; if it was murder, then I was in the direct line of fire.

Returning to my room, I locked the door, took off all my clothes except my drawers, and pulled the shade. I was dead tired, mostly because of the nearly sleepless night. I put my gun under my pillow and got into bed, thinking that the lock would be no great puzzle to anyone who was determined to get into my room.

Even though it was early, I dropped off to sleep at once. I woke suddenly with the knowledge that someone was in the room with me. Cold sweat broke out all over me. I lay motionless for only a few seconds, not sure what woke me. Maybe it was the key dropping to the floor, or the door squeaking. I moved my right arm slowly and carefully to my pillow and clutched the butt of my gun, all the time fighting to keep from panicking and rolling out of bed.

The room was too dark to see anything, but the feeling that someone else was in the room was overpowering. When I had the gun securely in my hand, I threw back the covers and rolled toward the wall farthest from the door. The bed squealed its disapproval, then I hit the floor with a thump just as a gunshot ripped a line of flame into the blackness. The bullet struck the wall directly above me. I pulled myself up to my knees and fired across the bed at the spot where the gunman had been standing, but he wasn't standing there by the time I got off the shot. He flung the door open and the lamplight from the hall washed into the room, but he was through the door before I had a chance to fire again.

I ran around the foot of the bed and into the hall. I was just in time to see a man's leg being drawn through an open window on the alley side of the building. I sprinted toward it as the night clerk raced up the stairs and doors banged open along the hall. People in their night clothes cautiously stuck their heads outside their rooms. By the time I reached the window and looked out, my assailant was nowhere to be seen. There was enough light from the street for me to see a roof of some kind below me. The drop had been an easy one for the man.

"What the hell's going on?" the night clerk demanded.

"Nothing, except that somebody just tried to kill me," I said.

The clerk motioned at the people who were looking from partly opened doors. The fact that I was in my drawers didn't bother me. If the women didn't want to see a nearly naked man, they could get to hell back into their rooms. I strode along the hall, the clerk trotting behind me. I went into my room and slammed the door, hoping to keep the clerk in the hall, but he caught the door, followed me inside, and then closed the door and stood against it.

I turned the light on and wheeled to face him. "Get out of here," I said. "I'm going back to bed."

He was not the clerk who had been on duty when I checked in. This fellow was a skinny, pasty-faced boy not over sixteen or seventeen. He didn't move. He just stared at me. I went around the bed and located the bullet hole the killer had made in the wall. It had been close, I thought, too damned close.

"Who are you?" the clerk demanded. "And why would anyone try to kill you the first night you're in town?"

"I'm Bob Norberg from Denver," I said. "I don't know why anyone would try to kill me. Now get out of here before I throw you out."

He hesitated, still eyeing me suspiciously as if I had done something wrong, then he turned and left the room. I picked the key up from the floor and locked the door again but I didn't think he'd come back tonight. At least I knew one thing. My opposition, Kirby or Wirt or whoever it was, did not believe in bluffing. He wanted to murder me.

Chapter IV

The following morning I was awakened from a deep sleep by a hammering on my door. The blinds were pulled down, so the room was dark and I had no idea what time it was. I staggered out of bed, groggy and thick-headed, and opened the door. A fat man with a star on his vest above his protruding belly pushed past me into the room without waiting for an invitation.

"You gonna sleep your life away, mister?" he asked in an insulting tone, as he crossed the room to the window and ran the shades up.

I yawned and rubbed my face as sunlight flooded into the room. I slowly regained a sense of knowing what was going on, and I didn't like it worth a damn. Sheriff or not, he didn't have the right to bull his way into my room and insult me.

"You the sheriff?" I asked.

"You bet I am. Sheriff Ed Allen. I'm the law in Tremont County." He stood with his back against the wall beside the window, his thumbs hooked under his belt. He stared at me as if I was a bug he might step on later after he decided what to do with me. "You're the Denver reporter who's sticking his nose into Tremont County business, ain't you?"

"I'm a Denver reporter. Bob Norberg. Tremont County's business belongs to more than Tremont County. Now, do you always walk into a room regardless of whether you're invited or not?"

"If I need to talk to a man, and I figured I needed to talk to

19

you," he snapped. "I hear you're here to look into the Susie Bowman affair. I'm telling you it's Tremont County's business and not Denver's, so you can pack your bag..."

"Now just hold on a minute." I guess I raised my voice, but I was fully awake by that time and getting damned sore. "You've got more pressing problems than telling me what you think about the Susie Bowman business. I was going to see you as soon as I had my breakfast. A man tried to kill me last night."

"That so?" He shrugged as if it didn't make much difference. "Now about your..."

I started walking toward him, mad enough to take his star away from him, then stopped. "I told you a man tried to kill me last night. Are you going to do anything about it?"

He seemed surprised. He pursed his lips and whistled tunelessly for a few seconds, then he said, "I don't see that I can do much about it. He's gone, ain't he?"

That was true enough. I had my temper under control by that time, and turned to the bureau and poured water into the bowl. "All right. Don't bother. I'll take care of my own problems."

"Good," he said. "Now a question occurs to me. You're in town less than twenty-four hours and someone tries to kill you. What have you done that would make a man try to do that?"

I washed my face and dried, my temper beginning to fray again. He tone indicated that I was the troublemaker, and not the killer. "Nothing," I said. "I want to know about Susie Bowman and the background to her trouble. I understand you're Ike Kirby's man. Looks to me as if you might know why somebody would try to kill me."

That made him mad. "I'm not Ike Kirby's man, and I sure as hell don't like the insinuation you're making. If Susie Bowman or anybody else breaks the law, I arrest them." He took a long breath, his jelly-like belly expanding and contracting with it. "I came up here to tell you that this Susie Bowman business is dynamite. We don't want folks worked up no more than they are now, and if your damned Denver paper starts kicking up dust, we'll have trouble, so get out of town and let us alone."

"All right," I said. "You've spoken your piece. Now I'll speak mine. I'm not leaving town until I get done finding out all I can about Susie, including going out to the Cove." I picked up my shaving brush and started working up a lather. "Suppose you get out of my room and let me dress."

He stood there for a good part of a minute scowling at me, then I guess he decided he couldn't do any more to change my mind, so he walked out. I slammed the door and shaved and dressed, all the time wondering what kind of trouble Allen expected to develop if the *Chronicle* kicked up more dust. There must be deeper feeling about Susie than I realized.

If she was the leader of the Cove ranchers, as I had been told, and if she was sent to the pen, they might give up and let Kirby have his winter range. On the other hand, if she was still around by fall when Kirby wanted to drive his herd into the Cove, there would probably be resistance and Kirby might be the one who would make trouble. Ed Allen, if my judgment of him was correct, wouldn't want trouble either way.

Some folks thought that keeping the peace and preventing trouble was the most important thing a man could do, regardless of the issues that were involved. I had a notion that the Reverend John Ross was that kind of man, but it seemed more likely that the sheriff had been bought and paid for by Ike Kirby. That led me to Judge Oscar Wirt.

As soon as I finished breakfast. I went to Wirt's office in the courthouse. It was nine o'clock by that time, so I figured he'd be in his office by then. When I entered, I found a man sitting at a desk who didn't look the way I had pictured Judge Oscar Wirt. For some reason, maybe just from the way he was reacting to the Susie Bowman case, I had built him up in my mind as an old man, bald-headed, pompous, and as tough as a boot heel.

Instead, this man, who stood up when I went in, was six feet tall or more, handsome, with dark brown hair and eyes, and a black, carefully clipped mustache, sinewy-muscled without an ounce of fat on him, and as bronze-faced as any cowboy.

"I'm looking for Judge Wirt," I said.

"You found him." H walked around the desk and held out his hand. "I'm guessing you're Bob Norberg from the *Denver Chronicle*. Reverend Ross told me about you."

He had a firm grip, a friendly manner, an outgoing personality, and although I had come into his office expecting to despise the man, I found myself instinctively liking him. He motioned me to a chair and, as I sat down, he resumed his seat behind his desk.

"I'm surprised," I said. "You don't look the way I thought a judge would look."

He laughed. "I can say the same about you. I'm not

21

familiar with the way Denver reporters look, but I wouldn't peg you for one."

"I suppose reporters and judges get stereotyped," I said. "I don't ordinarily dress this way. I'm wearing the work clothes I always wore when I used to go home to my dad's ranch in Wyoming. My boss said I'd be less conspicuous in Canby if I wore these clothes. Now I'm beginning to think he was wrong."

"It depends on what you plan to do," he said. "If you're going to stay in Canby, which I hope you won't, your clothes probably are a mistake."

"I plan to ride out to Smith's Cove," I said. "I want to talk to the people out there, particularly Susie Bowman." Wirt leaned back in his swivel chair, his hands folded across his lean stomach. I paused, wondering why he had said he hoped I didn't stay in Canby, so I asked him. "I'm curious about why you hope I won't stay in town."

"Because it might mean trouble for all of us if you do," he said. "The sheriff was just in and told me someone had tried to kill you last night. Believe me, Mr. Norberg, I deplore that. We all would prefer that you go back to Denver and give up this investigation simply because if you or anyone else keeps fanning the fire, we're going to have a good-sized flame going before we know it. I don't have any notion about who tried to kill you or why, but it illustrates the feeling that gripped the town during Susie's trial, and we will in all likelihood have it again when she's tried the second time."

"I guess I don't savvy that," I said.

"Let me explain a few things about this country." He eased his chair back down and leaned forward. "Originally Tremont County was cattle country and nothing else, with a few big outfits around town. Gradually small ranchers drifted into the valleys and pockets similar to Smith Cove, and I'm afraid they've eaten their share of other men's beef. Now we also have a large group of dry-land farmers who have taken up homesteads south of town. Their interests are different from either group of cattlemen, and they don't like them worth a damn."

He picked up a box of cigars from his desk, flipped the lid back and held the box out to me. I don't make a habit of smoking, but I like a good cigar occasionally. I took one, bit off the end, fired it, and found that it was a good cigar indeed. Wirt was silent until he got his going.

After puffing a moment, he went on, "Those of us in town

are interested in a good relationship with all three groups, because that's the only way we can have a prosperous community. The spirit of the old pioneer land is very close in this county. Both Sheriff Allen and I were worried about violence the first time Susie was tried. Her friends talked about breaking her out of jail if she was convicted, and sending her out of the country. The big cowmen talked about breaking the jail door down and hanging her.

"As it stands now we may really have that kind of violence when she's tried. The point is that if your paper or any other paper challenges the way the law in Tremont County operates, we'll have trouble sure, and nothing this side of an act of God would prevent it. Now if you go back to Denver and let us carry on our business with as little publicity as possible, we may be able to prevent bloodshed."

I puffed on my cigar and thought about it, but I just couldn't see that it made as much sense for me to get out of town as the Judge and the Reverend John Ross seemed to think. Finally I said, "If my paper tells the truth, I can't understand how it can add to the threat of violence."

"The way the truth is stated will have a great deal to do with what happens," he said. "There are some hotheads in the county who think they can make their own laws. The man who tried to kill you is an example. If he or someone else succeeds, that act of murder would focus the entire state's attention on this county. Along with the fact that I would hate to see you meet an untimely end, I don't want that kind of attention focused on us."

I didn't want to argue, so I let it go and asked, "There is one thing that jars me. Why have you made it so plain that Susie should be convicted?"

He held up a hand. "I can explain that in a few words. There was ample evidence submitted during the trial to convict Susie Bowman. I hate waste, and this second trial is a waste of both time and money, all because some bullheads on the jury were only interested in getting the woman off."

Wirt leaned forward. "I judge you to be a moral man. I think it would be an excellent idea for you to spend some time in Smith Cove and get acquainted with Susie. You will find her a very eccentric woman who flaunts the laws of God and man. I think she will offend you just as she offends the rest of us."

The more I heard about Susie Bowman, the more I was interested in meeting her, but I didn't pursue that with Judge

Wirt. I asked, "What can you tell me about Ike Kirby?"

Wirt's face lost his friendly expression. He said savagely, "He's the real problem in Tremont County. He should have lived fifty years ago. He's a Goddamned outlaw, Mr. Norberg. If he wasn't hellbent on having his way, we wouldn't be having this trouble."

That flabbergasted me. So Wirt wasn't in Kirby's pocket after all? But I didn't let the surprise I felt show in my face. I asked, "Will you explain that?"

"Actually Kirby doesn't spend much time in Tremont County," Wirt said. "His major holdings are in southern Wyoming and eastern Utah. He owns a house in Canby, which he uses when he travels from Wyoming to his Utah ranch, and vice versa. He does own one spread, Hatchet, on the Little Snake, which is not far from the entrance to Smith Cove. What he wants to do—and he's been working on this for several years—is to buy the Cove people out so he can use the Cove for winter range. They won't sell, so last fall he tried to drive his herd into the Cove anyhow."

Wirt pointed his forefinger as if it were a pistol. "That's where we're in a bind. Legally he has a right to use the open range in the Cove, but the ranchers there know that if he puts his herd onto that grass, there won't be enough for them. Legally I'd say the law is on his side, but if I had lived in the Cove as long as the Bowmans and some of the others have, I'd fight, too." He spread his hands. "So you see, Mr. Norberg, it's a very complex situation."

"What happened when he tried it last year?" I asked.

"It came close to war," Wirt said. "Every man and boy and some women met his outfit at the entrance into the Cove and turned his herd back. He wasn't there at the time, but he says this fall he will be, and he'll put his cattle into the Cove."

"If he has a small outfit on the Little Snake..." I began.

"It's a horse ranch, but mostly it's a stopping place for his cattle," Wirt interrupted. "He drives a herd from Utah to Rawlins to ship every fall. It's too long a drive through dry country and his steers lose too much weight. It would be worth thousands of dollars to him to be able to winter the herd in the Cove and drive to Rawlins the following spring."

"What has Susie Bowman's case got to do with Kirby's schemes?"

"Why, nothing," he said, as if surprised. "The sheriff had

the deadwood on her. Everybody's known for years that the Cove bunch has been stealing cattle from the big spreads. A couple of men, Ash Morck and Ned Rusk, are notorious rustlers, but the sheriff was never able to catch them in the act. Susie Bowman is probably just as bad, and Allen finally came up with the evidence on her." He rose, terminating the interview, then added, "The Cove bunch is a scummy lot, as you'll see if you spend some time with them."

I rose and shook hands, thanking him for his time, and left his office. It was going to take some thinking to sort things out in my mind, but one thing bothered the hell out of me. Judge Wirt was no friend of Ike Kirby, and by all odds he should have been.

Chapter V

I went directly to the office of the *Canby Weekly Herald*. I remembered seeing it the previous afternoon when I had explored the town, a tarpaper shack set on the west end of the business block, certainly no permanent monument to the power of the rural press. A firetrap if I ever saw one. Again I wondered, as I had so many times, how any small-town print shop survived.

I found the interior of the building similar to a dozen others I had visited in the last eight years. The general impression I received when I walked through the door was one of complete chaos. The room was littered with the press, the type stands, the desk with its piles of paper, wastebaskets that no one bothered to use, several spittoons, and stacks of different kinds and sizes of paper everywhere. In the back was a small heating stove.

The similarity to other small-town newspaper offices ended with this first glance. The editor was quite another matter. I thought I had seen all kinds of newspaper editors, but never one like this. He turned from the type stand where he had been standing and walked toward me when he heard the door open, wiping his ink-stained hands on his heavy apron. He was a gnome of a man with a wrinkled face that made him look a thousand years old, but his eyes belied the appearance of age. They were a bright blue, snapping with good humor and a zest for life.

"You're Bob Norberg," he said, as he extended a claw-like hand, his tone more a statement than a question.

"Correct," I said as we shook hands. "I guess news gets around."

"In a small town it does," he said, nodding. "I'm Clyde Gorman, Sid's brother."

"I'll be damned," I said, as shocked as I had ever been in my life. "Sid didn't tell me he had a brother here."

"Oh, he knew you'd find out." He pulled up a straight-backed chair and motioned to it as he turned his swivel chair and sat down. "I'm a little over a century older than Sid. Most of the family are dead. Just a sister who lives in Denver and the two of us. We don't see each other very often, mostly because I hate Denver and he never comes here, but we keep in touch. As a matter of fact, I'd say I am probably the reason for you being here."

I sat down and stared at the old man, finding it hard to grasp the fact that he was Sid's brother. I couldn't see the least bit of resemblance. I had never heard anything about Sid's family. I knew he was a bachelor, but it hadn't occurred to me that he had any family. It was just that we'd never had any occasion to talk about family, beyond the joshing he had always given me when I used to get back from my dad's ranch with a sunburn that hurt like hell. Sid was always business and that suited me.

"I'm so surprised I don't know what to say." I shook my head. "But what do you have to do with me being here?"

"I'm very interested in Susie Bowman's upcoming trial," he answered. "I have to be very middle-of-the-road, very circumspect in the way I report the fight—and that's what it is. If I took sides, as I've often been tempted to do, I wouldn't be alive twenty-four hours, and my building would be burned to the ground."

He gave me an elfish grin. "So I had a brainstorm. I started nagging Sid about a month ago, writing to him every few days and telling him what was happening in Tremont County. I told him that this case is of interest to the whole state, that it's a place where the Old West and its lawlessness still survives, and that he could deliver a blow for justice through the *Chronicle*." His grin became a chuckle and he added, "Besides, I told him he could blow Ike Kirby right out of the saddle. He hates Kirby like poison."

Sid had never indicated that to me, but maybe he thought

27

it was touchy ground, knowing that my father had suffered at Kirby's hands. I asked, "Will I do?"

"You'll do," he said, nodding. "Well, Sid wrote to me a day or so ago that he was sending you to Tremont County, and for me to cooperate, which I would have done anyhow. He said you were the best man he had for this type of assignment and that you could take care of yourself. I hope to hell you can, because your life will be in danger."

"It is already," I said. "A man tried to kill me last night in my hotel room."

Startled, he stared at me as if he could not believe it. He asked in a hoarse voice, "Any idea who?"

"No," I answered, and told him what had happened. That led to my talk with John Ross and his hasty visit with Judge Oscar Wirt. Then I said, "The killer must have known who I was from what Ross told Wirt, but I can't really think Ross wanted me murdered. Or Wirt, either, for that matter, so I can't quite make a pattern out of it."

"It's a pretty complicated relationship," he said slowly, "and although I've lived here a long time and I know all the people involved, I don't know for sure what's going on. But I'm like you. I can't really believe it was either Ross or Wirt, who are basically decent men. The only real scoundrel in the lot is Ike Kirby, although I have to admit that some of the Cove people are pretty miserable excuses for human beings."

"A while ago, when I was talking to Wirt," I said, "he acted downright mad at Kirby. Called him a Goddamned outlaw and said he should have lived fifty years ago."

"That's right. Kirby's cut from the same bolt of cloth that the Wyoming ranchers were, who invaded Johnson County thinking they had a right to hang everybody who was on their list. To Kirby there is no law except what he makes up according to his whims." He paused and scratched his chin, his gaze on the ceiling, then he added thoughtfully, "It is passing strange that the Judge would speak that way about Kirby."

"Are they good friends?"

"No, Kirby is not a good friend to anyone except himself," Gorman answered. "It's not a matter of being friends. The big cowmen stick together because their interests coincide. The little fry like the ones in the Cove are, by the very nature of things, their natural enemies. The Judge has a good-sized outfit up the Yampa and raises pure-bred Herefords, the best in the county. I don't think he's lost as much to the rustlers as some of the others have, but with him it's a matter of principle."

"Is that why he's so set on convicting Susie?"

"Partly," Gorman said. "You see, it's no secret that folks in the Cove eat outsiders' beef. It's been going on for years, but there is more of it now than there used to be. You add it all up and it becomes a considerable loss. When the sheriff found that hide on Susie's fence, it was the first hard evidence they had, so they decided to make an example out of her. Then there's another thing. Susie is a pretty salty-tongued young woman. When Wirt told her there would be another trial, and to stay in the county, she let go at him with some very choice words. He will never forgive her."

I nodded. "He's obviously a proud man."

"It's safe to say that no one ever talked to him that way before."

"How about that hide? Wasn't it a frame-up?"

"Probably. The odds are ten to one simply because Susie is no fool, and only a fool would steal a heifer, butcher it, and leave the hide on the fence for anyone to see. But how do you prove it?"

I nodded. "There was Chip Malone's testimony."

"It's the only defense she's got. He swears she couldn't have done it without him knowing it. But you see, Chip was raised by Susie's parents and he lived out there until a year ago. I guess his testimony didn't count for much because he's a biased witness, but it raised enough doubt that some of the jurors wouldn't vote for conviction." He paused, looking at me as if he wasn't sure of the truth of what he was going to say, but he continued: "It is my belief that neither Wirt nor the sheriff knows it was a plant."

I rose. "I came in to ask if I could go over your old copies of the *Herald* for the last five years. I think I know the story, but before I go out to the Cove, I'd like to see if there's anything I've missed."

"Help yourself." He pointed to a long shelf on the far wall that was piled high with newspapers. "The two piles on the left are what you want."

He pushed the mess of papers that was on his desk into a pile at one end and rose as he added, "The light isn't all that it ought it be, but you'll have to make do."

On a cloudy day it would have been dim   the only

artificial light a small bulb hanging high above the desk, but today was very bright so I didn't need the electric light. I did wonder what Gorman did on gray winter days when it would be close to dark inside the long room with its small, fly-specked windows.

I carried a pile of old *Herald*s from the shelf and laid them on the desk, sat down, pulled my chair up and set to work. I stayed on it until noon, learning very few hard facts I didn't already know, but I picked up some tidbits that filled in a few details and gave me a better picture of the Cove community.

Alec Bowman, Susie's and Janey's father, had died three years ago. He had been the community leader, and his death and funeral received a headline and a two-column story. After that there were a number of brief items about Susie and Janey, and all were stated in a strange manner. Gorman never said that Susie and Janey visited in Canby. Invariably it was Susie Bowman of Smith Cove who was visiting in Canby. Then another sentence reported that she was accompanied by her sister Janey, as if Janey was an afterthought.

Inasmuch as Susie was the one who had been held for stealing the heifer, and Janey was never mentioned, I sensed that Gorman was reacting in the same manner others did. I knew I should be reading something into it beyond the fact that Susie was the dominant personality, but I wasn't sure what it was.

I found many notices of weddings, births and deaths among the Cove people, and now and then an announcement of a dance in the hall over the general store. Then I came to the story about Susie's arrest which Sheriff Allen made in person, the finding of the hide, and then the trial. Nothing new, but one thing did strike me. The article ended with a direct quote from Judge Wirt to the effect that there had been sufficient evidence presented to the jury by the prosecution to justify a guilty verdict, and that he would see to it that she was tried again and again until she was found guilty.

When I left the newspaper office to get my dinner in the hotel dining room, I thought about the Judge's statement, which seemed completely out of keeping with the theory that a judge must be impartial. I had no way of knowing whether he had made decisions during the trial that hurt Susie's case or not, but I didn't see how he could keep from it, feeling as strongly as he did about Susie's guilt.

Not being an expert on legal matters, I wasn't certain of

my ground, but it struck me that the Judge's statement was sufficient to secure a dismissal of the charges, or at least give the defense lawyer grounds for demanding that Judge Wirt be disqualified. A judge from outside Tremont County would certainly give Susie a fairer trial.

As soon as I finished eating, I walked along Main Street to the Red Front Livery Stable and found Chip Malone currying a fine-looking bay gelding. I said, "That's a good-looking animal."

"The best we've got," he agreed. "If you're looking for a riding horse, I'll make you a good deal. I'd have to see the boss, but he don't usually argue with me on a horse trade. I do most of the buying and selling for him."

"I thought you were working here just through the winter and spring," I said, "and that you were looking for a riding job."

"I am," he said, "but the chances of me finding one are about zero. The fact is I'm blackballed by the Tremont County cattlemen because I testified for Susie. It comes down to leaving the county or working here. I figger I'll hang on till after Susie's trial, then I'll be riding on."

He stepped out of the stall and laid his currycomb on a shelf along the wall. "I've got a half-assed offer from a ranch across the Wyoming line just out of Hicks, but I dunno if I want it or not. Chances are I'll get beefed if I take it. I'm more unpopular up there with the law than I am in Canby."

I was curious about that, curious enough to ask why, though I had a hunch I shouldn't, it being a private matter. Still, he'd opened the subject up, so I thought he couldn't get too sore about me asking.

"Oh, I had a run-in with the marshal one time," Chip said. "He's a tough hand. The cowmen brought him in a year ago from some mining camp in Colorado where they were having a strike, and the mine owners had hired him to murder a couple of union leaders. Nobody would prove it, but that sure as hell is what happened. I guess you've heard there has been an increase of rustling lately, and the cowmen thought this bastard could stop it. They hired him and made him a deputy on both sides of the line."

"Did he stop it?"

"Of course not. He don't get out of town much. Claims they'll come to him. Hicks is a tough town. It ain't changed much, and I guess the truth is the marshal ain't real popular with the people. The Wild Bunch used to hang around up there and everybody loved 'em." He shrugged. "Him being popular or not wouldn't save my hide if he had a chance to plug me."

I started to ask about renting the bay, but stopped in the middle of my sentence. A man came in and walked along the runway to us, a man that sent a chill raveling down my spine. I knew I was jumping to a mighty hasty conclusion, but I had a hunch that this was the fellow who tried to murder me last night.

Chapter VI

I'm not sure exactly why I pegged this man for the assassin who had been in my room the previous night except that he was big, and the one impression I had of the gunman was that he was big. But then I doubt that there is ever any why to a hunch. I've had them often enough, and although I never kept a count, I'd say about seventy-five percent of mine turned out to be correct.

One thing was sure. I didn't like this fellow. He was arrogant as hell. He came along the runway with the determined stride of a man who would not be deterred from his goal by God or man. He didn't hang back because I was talking to Chip, but moved in without acknowledging my presence.

"I want to rent this horse for a week." He handed Chip a gold coin. "Maybe longer, but if I decide to keep him for another week or more, I'll let you know. Saddle him up."

Chip shot a glance at me as he pocketed the coin, then started to saddle the bay. I had a good chance to study the man as he stood in the runway a few feet back of the stall and watched Chip. He still acted as if I was just part of the scenery.

He was, I thought, at least a quarter Indian. He had high cheekbones, a beak of a nose, and thin lips that held no hint of a smile or good humor. His hair that showed under his worn, black Stetson was black, his eyes were brown, and his skin was dark—not the bronze of a cowboy, but the dark hue of a man who was born with skin the color it was now. I guess you couldn't say it was the copper-brown of an Indian, but it was damned close. He was about six feet two, I judged. He must have weighed two hundred pounds, and I don't think an ounce of it was fat.

Chip backed the gelding out of the stall and handed the reins to the man. He mounted and rode into the street without another word. I said, "I'll be back," and followed the man into the street, curious about the direction he'd take, but he didn't leave town. He rode to the hotel, tied up, and went in.

I stopped in front of a jewelry store about thirty feet from the hotel entrance and waited. I didn't watch the time, but he must have been in the hotel ten minutes or more before he came out carrying a Winchester and a bedroll which he tied behind his saddle. He was wearing a gun belt, a revolver in the holster. He stepped into the saddle and rode out of town toward the west.

For several minutes I stood there watching him until he was out of sight, the thought occurring to me that this fellow could be the Van Tatum Sid Gorman had mentioned, who had talked to Kirby, Judge Wirt, and a third man in Denver. Not that it would make any difference in my going to the Cove, but it might after I got there.

If I was guessing right in suspecting this man of trying to kill me in my hotel room, I could count on it happening again after I reached the Cove. On the other hand, he hadn't come here to kill me, because no one had known I was going to be here when the three men had met in the hotel room. The decision to get me out of the way had been made after I had come to Canby, so the intended victim who had brought Tatum to Tremont County must be someone living in the Cove.

On impulse as much as anything, I walked down the street to the Western Union office and wired Sid Gorman, asking for a description of Van Tatum, then I returned to the Red Front Livery Stable. Apparently Chip had finished his chores, because he was dozing in the tack room when I went in.

"Learn anything?" Chip asked.

"He took the road west out of town," I said. "Is that the way you go to Smith's Cove?"

He straightened up. "Yeah. You think that's where he's headed?"

"Just a guess," I said. "Did he give you his name?"

"He came in yesterday and looked the horses over," Chip said. "Told me his name was Vic Tate and he was a horse buyer from Rawlins." He gestured as if thrusting the idea away. "Hell, he's no horse buyer. He's a killer. I know the breed. I've seen enough of 'em when I lived in the Cove. It was a hideout for 'em, and had been for years. The Wild Bunch hung out there a couple of winters. Susie had a crush on Cassidy. I won't forget that because I was jealous of him. I couldn't do much about it, being just a kid. Not that I'm saying the Wild Bunch were killers, though some of 'em were."

"Vic Tate..."

I said the two words to myself more than to Chip. I had often heard that when men change their names, they pick names that give them the same initials. If this man was Tatum, that was exactly what he had done. Well, I'd probably find out when I heard from Sid Gorman.

"That's what the man said." Chip reached for tobacco and paper. "The name mean anything to you?"

"Nothing," I said. "Well, he got the horse you were going to give me."

"Oh, we've got plenty of horses, some good, some bad." Chip sealed his smoke and fired it. "Now there's a little black gelding back there in the corral named Prince. He ain't got quite the easy gait the bay has, but he'll do fine."

I smelled a king-sized rat from the way Chip was taking his time with his cigarette and not looking at me. I said, "You're not the kind of jayhoo who would give a greenhorn a horse that would dump him on his hind-end the first time he got aboard, are you?"

"Hell, no!" He laughed, as if suddenly realizing I wasn't as much of a greenhorn as he'd thought. "Oh, Prince is a little foxy first thing in the morning, but after about three jumps he's fine. If you don't want him, I've got some crowbaits here that will probably get you to the Cove."

"I'll try him," I said. "I hope to get work in the Cove. You think Susie Bowman would hire me?"

"Why, hell, man, she'd ..." He stopped and chewed on his lower lip. "She might, at that, if you can cut the mustard, but I ain't sure you can take what she hands out. Janey's a hell of a good cook and you'll get along fine with her, but Susie?" He shook his head. "I dunno. You just never can guess what she's going to do next."

"I'll try it," I said. "She can't any more than fire me."

"You gonna tell her you're a reporter?" I nodded, and he

35

added, "Then she'll work your ass off."

"I'll take a chance," I said. "I'll be here in the morning right after breakfast."

I returned to the *Herald* and finished the last year following the trial. I didn't learn anything more except the few items that referred to the increase of rustling and horse stealing, and a quote from Ike Kirby to the effect that he knew how to deal with thieves—that if a man waited for the law to take its course, a cowman would go broke.

It was, I thought, a direct slap at Sheriff Allen and Judge Wirt. Maybe they weren't in Kirby's pocket as completely as I had thought. Or if they had been, he'd discarded them.

I found one more item that interested me. It told about the appointment of Al Galt as the Hicks town marshal and deputy sheriff for both Carbon County in Wyoming and Tremont County in Colorado. He would be in a position to run down rustlers and horse thieves in both counties, the article said, and it was hoped that he would restore law and order in Hicks.

As I carried the newspapers back to the shelf where I had found them, Clyde Gorman asked, "You find what you were looking for?"

"Part of it, anyhow," I answered. "What's your judgment on Al Galt?"

"He's a hangover from the old days," Gorman said, "the kind of man who is worse than the outlaws he's supposed to arrest. He was Kirby's idea, but he's turned out to be too lazy to change anything up there, except to kill a couple of troublemakers who really weren't that bad but were supposed to be resisting arrest."

I picked up the notes I had made, folded them, and stuffed them into my coat pocket. I said, "I still don't know why Sid is as emotionally involved as he is. Even with you working on him, it doesn't seem a big enough case for him to give so much space in the *Chronicle* to a trial being held three hundred miles from Denver."

Gorman busied himself filling his pipe and lighting it. Finally he said, "It's quite a love story. It's Susie's mother, Freda. She died just when the girls were entering their teens. Sid used to be in love with her when they were living in Missouri and weren't much more than kids. He didn't have any money, so he couldn't ask her to marry him. Of course he hoped she'd wait for him, but Alec Bowman came along. He was pretty well fixed, so when he proposed, she accepted him. I guess she thought it would be years before Sid could support her and she was right.

"Alec and Freda moved west and finally settled out there in the Cove, when Canby wasn't more than a post office and a store. The Cove was a pretty wild piece of country then. It had been a hangout for outlaws, and was for years after the Bowmans settled there, but Alec always got along with them.

"Alec's problem was with Susie. Janey grew up to be a lady, but Susie was independent and strong-willed even when she was little. After Freda died, Susie became a regular hellion, but the funny thing is that everybody out there loves her.

"Well, Sid never got over loving Freda and, as you know, he never married. One reason he won't come here is because he can't bear the emotion that it raises in him. Seems that it brings everything back to him. Now I consider that crazy, especially coming from a hardhead like Sid, but I guess we all have our vulnerable areas."

He puffed for a moment, then took the pipe out of his mouth. "Don't ever mention to Sid that I told you all of this. He'd never speak to me again. Even though he won't come here and he doesn't want to meet the girls, he's anxious to keep tabs on them, so I write everything I hear about them. He doesn't want Susie to go to prison, so he'll do what he can. Sending you out here is all he can do right now."

It took me a moment to absorb all of this. The Sid Gorman I was hearing about didn't seem much like the tough newspaperman I worked for. I was seeing a side of him I did not know existed. I started to leave and I was still thinking about it when I reached the door.

"Anything else I can do for you, just speak up," Gorman said. "I can be very brave through the pages of the *Chronicle*, but I'm a coward when it comes to writing for my own *Herald*."

"After the man tried to kill me the other night," I said, "I can understand why you don't kick the roof off through your newspaper."

He stared at his pipe that he held in his hand. "You know, Norberg, there was a time, when I was young and filled with piss and vinegar, that I would have gone after Kirby hammer and tongs, but I don't have the guts any more."

"I'm riding out to the Cove tomorrow," I said. "I'm going to ask Susie for a job."

He had put his pipe back into his mouth, and now I

thought he was going to swallow it. He yanked it out of his mouth and sputtered, "My God, man, do you know what you're asking for?"

"No," I said, "but I'll find out."

One thing was sure, I thought, as I walked back to the hotel. No living, breathing woman could possibly fit the image of Susie Bowman that had been developing ever since I had arrived in Canby.

Chapter VII

I was surprised when I entered the hotel and found the Reverend John Ross sitting in the lobby. He was the last man I wanted to see, but I didn't have much choice in the matter. He jumped up the instant he saw me and ran to me, his hand extended.

"I've been waiting to see you, Mr. Norberg," he said, talking rapidly as if he couldn't get the words out fast enough. "I've got to apologize and say how pleased I am that you are alive. When I talked to Judge Wirt after I saw you yesterday, I had no idea that it might lead to an attempt on your life."

I was astonished, to say the least. I said, "Let's go into the dining room and have a cup of coffee. You do have an explanation to make."

"Yes, indeed," he said heartily. "I know I do. Yes, I'll be delighted to have a cup of coffee with you."

He led the way into the dining room. As I followed, I was wondering just how much he would admit and how much blame he would place on Judge Wirt. As near as I could tell, both Ross and Wirt were respected men in Canby, and I didn't think Kirby was.

Ross led the way to a table near the window. We sat down and a waitress took our order, but before Ross could say anything, I asked, "I have a question or two I want answered. First, was Ike Kirby in town yesterday afternoon?"

"Yes, but I had no intention of informing him directly or indirectly of your presence in Canby."

"Do you think he was the one responsible for the attempt on my life?"

"Yes," he answered quickly. "Perhaps I have no right to say that. I don't have a shred of proof. I only know I had nothing to do with it, and I can't believe that Judge Wirt did. He doesn't want you in town and he doesn't want any Denver newspaper nitpicking and criticizing the way we solve our problems, but murder . . . No, I can't believe that of him."

"But do you think he went to Kirby after you talked to him?"

"Yes, I know he did," Ross said. "He told me he did. Now I'd like to make the explanation I came here to make." Our coffee came and we spooned sugar into our cups. As soon as the waitress left, he went on hurriedly, "I told you yesterday that Judge Wirt expected a Denver reporter to come to Canby. I told you I couldn't tell you how he knew, but now I'm going to tell you, because there has been too much secrecy, too much covering up. I'm tired of having a man like Ike Kirby dictating to us. We owe him nothing. Actually he pays very little in taxes in Tremont County. To him it is simply a highway over which he drives his herd to the railroad at Rawlins. Smith's Cove is a potential winter grazing ground which he wants in spite of anybody else's rights."

He paused to take a drink of coffee and catch his breath. I was more surprised than ever now, and my respect for John Ross went up a couple of notches. I began to suspect that here was a rebel, under the established ministerial robe which he habitually wore.

"Clyde Gorman told the Judge that his brother Sid was sending a reporter here," Ross went on. "What I'm saying is not meant to be critical of Mr. Gorman. It's just that a few of us who love our community find the situation intolerable and we exchange confidences. He actually wanted you here, arguing that publicity will help us and hurt Kirby. The rest of us disagreed. We want to work out our problems ourselves. I don't know if you can understand this or not, but those of us who live in small, outlying counties are not very fond of Denver, which has the bulk of the population and the lion's share of political power in the state.

"I guess we're sort of country cousins, you might say, and we have felt that the Denver newspapers notice us only if they find a sensational story out here that will increase their circulation. We resent that, Mr. Norbert, just as we resent the fact that we do not get our fair share of road improvements and school funds and the like."

I was familiar with this feeling, because I had run into it before in rural areas of the state, so it did not surprise me to hear it from Ross. However, it didn't seem to have much to do with the attempt on my life, beyond the fact that I was from Denver and Denver wasn't liked, therefore I fell heir to the bitterness the Canby people felt toward Denver.

Ross took a sip of coffee, then hurried on, "What I'm trying to say is that I went to Judge Wirt with the information that you were in town to investigate the Susie Bowman business. I only confirmed what he expected to happen, but I thought he should know. Now what he said to Kirby, or what Kirby did, is unknown to me.

"Actually, Mr. Norberg, we resent Kirby's influence in county affairs. He's an aggressive, self-centered, lawless man who takes all he can get and gives as little as he can. I warned you that you would not be safe here because I knew he might try to harm you. However, I did not think he would resort to murder.

"I also want to say that we are ashamed of Smith's Cove because there are known rustlers who live there and are protected by their neighbors. We would like to get rid of them, to give Tremont County a better name if nothing else. We are also ashamed of Susie Bowman's improper conduct and the way she flaunts her unladylike actions. If she is guilty of stealing that heifer, as Judge Wirt believes, she should be punished."

He rose, leaving half of the coffee in his cup. He extended his hand, adding, "I was not able to rest after I heard about the attempt on your life. Again I say I hope you will return to Denver. You know by now as well as I do that you are not safe here."

I got up, shook his hand, and then he whirled and walked out of the dining room. I stared at his back until he disappeared into the lobby, wondering if he actually believed that Wirt had nothing to do with the attempt on my life.

When I finished my coffee, I left the dining room and paused at the desk to ask where Fred Pherson's office was. He had been Susie Bowman's lawyer and I wanted to see him before I left town. I had a strong feeling that he had not been as interested in getting an acquittal for Susie as a defense attorney should have been, that the businessmen of Canby tended to hang

41

together and work for a common goal, and maybe, just maybe, Judge Oscar Wirt dictated what that goal should be.

"Pherson?" the clerk said, eyeing me suspiciously. "What do you want with him?"

This stirred my anger enough to make me want to grab his coat lapels and shake him until his liver quivered. I didn't. I fisted my hands and leaned across the desk and asked, "Now what the hell business is it of yours?"

Maybe he read my mind. He backed up and said, "Sorry. You'll find his office over the Canby Hardware. It's a block to your right when you leave the hotel."

As I stepped into the street, the sour thought crossed my mind that everybody in town knew by now who I was and why I was in Canby, and nobody but Clyde Gorman and Chip Malone wanted me here. I suspected that Fred Pherson would turn out the same way. Whether or not this attitude stemmed from Ike Kirby's influence was a question in my mind. I didn't think he was that popular, or that powerful. Judge Wirt was. There was no doubt of that.

Still, I couldn't really lay it at Wirt's door. I thought about my conversation with the Reverend John Ross. His resentment of Denver's political and business power was typical, and the hostility I was running into might be caused by that more than the influence of any one man.

My hunch about Fred Pherson was right. He was just getting ready to lock up when I entered his office. He stared at me, scowling. I asked, "Are you Fred Pherson?"

"I'm Pherson," he said curtly.

I knew right then he'd guessed who I was before I volunteered my name. I said, "I believe you were Susie Bowman's attorney when she was tried for stealing a heifer."

"That's right."

He stood beside his desk, his hat on his head, the scowl furrowing his forehead. He was a weak man, I thought, with a receding chin and a bald spot on top of his head as big as my hand. He was about fifty, short and paunchy, with a large, reddish-brown mole on his upper lip. I knew I was wasting my time asking him questions, but I decided to go ahead as long as I was there.

"I'm interested in Miss Bowman's case," I said. "It's no secret that Judge Wirt has said that there was sufficient evidence to convict her, that she would be tried until she was found guilty.

Isn't that sufficient grounds to ask for a dismissal of the case, or at least to disqualify Judge Wirt?"

"No."

"Or ask for a change of venue?" I pressed. "Obviously she will not get a fair trial in Tremont County in Judge Wirt's court. His mind is made up."

"No," he said again.

That was all. No explanation, no apologies, no nothing. Just plain, one-syllable no. I looked at him for a moment and shook my head. Susie had been hard-put to have hired a lawyer like Fred Pherson. I said, "Sorry to have taken your time."

I turned and left the room. As I walked back to the hotel through the warm, late-afternoon sunshine, I told myself that Pherson was the kind of man who could be intimidated by Wirt, and that he had probably done a half-assed job defending Susie. I was going to find out why she had hired him, and if she would hire him again for her second trial.

I decided to have my supper then and write out my dispatch to the *Chronicle*. I had a good deal to write about this time—nothing concrete, but there was no doubt about the attitude of the community toward me and the publicity that would result from my being here.

The chances were that if the *Chronicle* played the case up, emphasizing the angle that the lawless Old West still lived in Trement County, the other Denver newspapers would pick it up and Canby would become the most publicized small town in Colorado.

That probably was what Wirt and the other town fathers feared. For the first time I could at least partially understand how they felt. They probably would encourage the "right" kind of publicity, the positive kind that would encourage outsiders to invest their money here, but the kind of story I'd be writing wouldn't do that.

One thing was sure. I'd talked to enough men in Canby. All I wanted to do was to be on my way in the morning to Smith's Cove, but I didn't have my druthers. I was halfway through supper when a man came into the dining room and stopped, his gaze moving from one table to another until his eyes were pinned on me. I don't know how he knew who I was unless I had been described to him. Or maybe he simply recognized me as a stranger and guessed I was Bob Norberg. Anyhow, he strode directly to my table with the determined stride of a man who

43

would move a mountain if it blocked his path. It didn't take the seventh son of a seventh son to know this was Ike Kirby.

I kept on eating, pretending I didn't know he had stopped across the table from me and that he was staring down at me as if waiting for me to acknowledge his presence. I kept right on eating until he said, "You're the Denver reporter, ain't you?"

I looked up, chewing on a mouthful of steak. I took a good look at him and I recognized the validity of the statement that he should have been born fifty years ago. He was not a big man, but there was a sense of power about him, a sort of unflinching drive that said louder than words that nothing could stop him. He had red hair and a bristly red mustache, pale blue eyes that reminded me of two cold, highly polished stones, and a jutting jaw that, if it truly represented what tradition said it was supposed to, told me that here was a very hard man indeed.

"I'm from the *Chronicle*," I said. "Do you read it, Mr. Kirby?"

This stopped him for a moment, perhaps making him wonder how I knew who he was, but I didn't divert him as much as I had hoped. He ignored my question. Instead of answering me, he said in a clipped tone, as if he was stating some great, cosmic law, "You have been told to leave town. You're still here. Why?"

I rose and pushed back my chair. I wished I had my gun. I couldn't see that Kirby carried one, but I had the crazy feeling that here was a man who was capable of killing me in cold blood and then, appearing in Judge Wirt's court, have the case thrown out as justifiable homicide.

"I'm still here because I'm going to fry you, Mr. Kirby," I said. "You're going to be known all over the Rocky Mountain area as a man who flouts the law and insists on getting his own way by inspiring fear in the Tremont County authorities, or by using his financial power, or by murder. I shall not forget that you tried to have me killed last night."

His face turned as crimson as the wattles of a Rhode Island Red rooster. He didn't sputter, but he swallowed a couple of times. If he'd had a gun, I think he would have killed me then and there. Or if I'd been a smaller man, he would have assaulted me, but Ike Kirby was a man who considered the odds and never lost control.

After a few seconds, he said, "I did order a man to scare you into leaving town, but I did not instruct him to kill you."

By this time everyone in the dining room was watching us. Even the clerk had left his desk and was standing in the doorway staring at me, as if he could not believe what he was hearing.

I waited a few seconds to let the tension build, then I said slowly and deliberately, "I know where I was in bed, I know the route the bullet took, and I know I would have been killed if I had remained where I was. I am alive only by the grace of God and the fact that I moved when I did, therefore I can safely say, Mr. Kirby, that you are a Goddamned liar."

If his face could have been any redder, it would have. He moistened his lips with the tip of his tongue, and said in a low voice, "You have just committed suicide, my friend."

He turned and walked out with the same determined stride he had used to come to my table. I sat down and watched him until he disappeared into the lobby, and I thought that if he was my friend, I could stand having a lot of enemies.

I went up to my room and wrote out my dispatch for the day. I was scared. I guess I never was more scared in my life. I didn't know how or when Kirby would try again, but there was no doubt in my mind that he would. I didn't leave the hotel to mail my dispatch to Denver that night. I moved the bureau against the door so it would have taken considerable effort to get into the room, then I went to bed with my gun under my pillow.

Chapter VIII

As soon as I finished breakfast the following morning, I walked to the Western Union office and found a wire from Sid Gorman. He gave me the description I wanted of Van Tatum: tall, well-built, dark-skinned, high cheekbones, black hair, and dark brown eyes. The last words were: "known killer but never convicted."

I stuck the telegram into my pocket and walked back to the hotel. I couldn't have asked for a better description of Van Tatum. So Vic Tate was the killer Tatum. Chip Malone had pegged him right. The man had tried to kill me here in Canby. Well, he undoubtedly would try again in the Cove, if that was where he had gone, and I had every reason to think it was. I can't say I felt any better, even though I had to keep in mind that I was not the primary target.

I gathered up my gear, paid my hotel bill, and walked to the stable. Chip Malone had saddled the black gelding he called Prince and a leggy bay with a star in his forehead. He said as soon as he saw me, "Norberg, I don't know if you're the bravest man I ever met or just a plain idiot." He nodded at a lantern-jawed man who stepped out of a nearby stall, and added, "Norberg, meet my boss, Miles Hess. He's gonna run the stable while I'm gone."

Hess shook hands, then stepped back and gravely looked me over. He said, "He don't look like an idiot, Chip, so he must be a very brave man."

I didn't care for this conversation. I didn't say anything, but wheeled and stepped into the saddle. I had forgotten what

Malone had said about Prince being a little foxy, but I was instantly reminded. He went off the ground the instant I settled into the saddle. At least he gave me a fighting chance. I hung on, although I'm not sure how. He came down in what was to me a spine-cruncher. He did a little dance that seemed mild after the first jump and, finding I was still in the saddle, went down the runway and into the street on a dead run.

I managed to turn him west and let him go for a quarter of a mile or more. By that time he decided I was going to be with him for a while, so he stopped and turned his head to look at me to see what kind of a character he had on his back.

I was still hurting, but in spite of myself, I laughed. "You son of a bitch," I said. "You willing to live in peace now?"

I thought he nodded his head. I rode him all the rest of the time I was in Tremont County and he didn't give me any more trouble. In fact, he turned out to be a hell of a good horse, easy-gaited and fast when he needed to be, and I think the smartest animal I ever forked.

When I looked back, I saw Malone jogging toward me, a big grin on his face. When he reached me, he said, "I see you and Prince have made up."

"Yeah," I said. "I forgot what you said about him being a little foxy first thing in the morning, but he reminded me." Malone fell in beside me and rode on for a mile or so before I said, "Would you mind telling me what you meant about me being an idiot or a brave man. I don't feel like I'm either one."

"I guess you've been around small towns enough to know that whatever happens in a public place, or gets talked about, is passed on to everyone. It didn't take long for me to hear how you talked to Kirby. Now, I ain't one to defend him to nobody."

He shot a glance at me, then added, "I've got reason to hate the bastard, but I wouldn't talk to him face to face the way you done. He'll kill you, Norberg. He won't pull the trigger, but he'll see that it's done."

"He told me I had committed suicide." I thought about it a minute, then I went on, "I figgered I didn't have much to lose. He tried to kill me once before, so I knew he'd try again. I didn't want him to think he was sending me back to Denver with my tail between my legs. I've always had a notion that men like Kirby respect a man who stands up to them."

"You might be right," Chip said. "Nobody in this community has stood up to him, not even Judge Wirt."

47

"I don't savvy why you decided to go with me," I said. "I'm glad to have your company and I need a guide, but you hadn't mentioned it before."

"I figgered you'd need looking after," he said, staring straight ahead. "I pegged you for a lamb among wolves when you first showed up in Canby, but I may be wrong about that. Besides, I wanted to go to the Cove. Susie can use an extra hand for a few days and I was getting cabin fever in that damned stable. I'm tired of shoveling horse manure. I need a little wind in my face. I've been thinking about going up to Hicks and seeing about that riding job that was offered me."

That was all understandable. I'd had trouble figuring out why a free soul like Chip Malone had hung on to a livery-stable job. I knew it didn't pay big wages. Chip seemed to be a typical cowboy, and cowboys I had known would have struck out across the country looking for a job as soon as the weather warmed up, but I didn't say anything. It was Chip's business and I wasn't fixing to give him any of my wisdom.

We rode about five miles out of Canby, then angled off to the northwest, following a road through the sagebrush that was little more than two wheel ruts. It was a big country with mountains ahead to our left, and more to the right, and I had a hunch that the Cove was down there somewhere between them.

We had been silent for about an hour when Chip burst out, "Oh, hell, Norberg, you're a city dude, but you're a purty smart hombre. I don't suppose I'm fooling you a damned bit. The truth is I want to see Susie. I ain't been out there all winter and she's only been to town once. Maybe she won't let me sleep with her, but then again she might. I never know how she's gonna feel. If she wants it, she's the best woman in bed you ever seen. When she doesn't, she'll knock your head off if you try. She'll take you on once anyhow, just to see how good you are."

He glanced at me again. "I guess I just don't know how much a man should take off a woman, but I've taken a lot off Susie Bowman. I've been in love with her since we were kids. She won't marry me. She just don't want to be saddled with one man, though I don't think she's got any around she likes more than me. Well, I got so I couldn't stand it. You see, I had her on a limited basis, you might say, but I wanted all or nothing. That's why I moved out and came to town."

He began to roll a cigarette, his hands trembling a little. He was worked up just telling me about it, and I was surprised that he'd told me as much as he had. Maybe it did him good to share his problem with someone else, and, too, maybe he thought I'd better know something about Susie before I met her. I was glad to hear all he wanted to tell me. It wasn't the kind of thing I could use in a story I'd write for the *Chronicle*, but it did help me understand this strange woman I'd come here to write about.

"It's real peculiar how a family could have twins with one of 'em turning out like Janey, sweet and good and wanting to live a woman's life and never giving her folks no trouble, and Susie who was a hell-raiser when she was growing up. Her mother was a real lady, the kind who was offended by the old-fashioned name of Smith's Hole, so Alec Bowman changed the name to Smith's Cove. She wanted daughters and she wanted 'em to be ladies. She got the daughters, but she got only one lady. Janey turned out the way her mother wanted her to, but right from the first Susie had to have her own way.

"I reckon Susie should have been a boy. She was her daddy's girl. She could ride before she could walk. As soon as she was big enough, she went with him everywhere he'd let her. She finished the eighth grade in the Cove school but barely passed while Janey was a perfect student. They sent the girls to Canby to go to high school, and boarded 'em with a nice old lady who was supposed to ride herd on 'em, but she gave up on Susie her freshman year, so her folks sent her back East to a female 'finishing school,' I guess they called it. Her mother had gone there when she was a girl.

"Well, I guess she gave 'em fits back there, disgracing the dean of the school. At least the dean, who was a stuffy old woman, thought so. Susie ran away to find a horse she could ride. She thought up pranks that only a boy should think of. The dean wound up wiring Alec to come and get her as soon as he could. I'll never forget the day she got home. She didn't stop to kiss her mama or speak to me or Janey, but ran across the yard and got on a horse bareback and took off at a dead run. After about ten minutes she came back, jumped off the horse, kissed her mama, kissed me, kissed Janey and said this was heaven and she'd just come out of hell. Alec told me he'd paddled her ass good when he got back there, but she never mentioned it to me and never held it against him."

Chip finished his cigarette, ground it out, and tossed it away. "The thing I don't like about Susie is that she don't have

49

no more modesty than a bitch dog, but damn it, on the other
hand, she's got a heart as big as a washtub and more guts than
any man I know.

"She was responsible for turning Kirby's herd back last
year when his foreman tried to drive it into the Cove. A bunch
who lived in the Cove had word the herd was coming. They were
hunkered down back of some rocks waiting for them. Susie was
giving orders and nobody argued, not even Ash Morck or Ned
Rusk. She rode out to meet the herd and told Kirby's ramrod
straight out that they'd get shot to hell, cowhands and cows
both, if they kept coming. Well, sir, he took a good look at
Susie—and she can look plenty mean and tough when she wants
to—and he turned the herd around and wintered 'em there on
Kirby's spread, which meant buying a lot of hay and losing some
during the winter."

"He'll try again this fall, won't he?" I asked.

"Sure he will," Chip said. "He'll be there in person, too.
He's a lot tougher than his foreman. I figure that's the reason
he's hellbent on sending her to the pen this summer. Without
her, I don't think the Cove men will fight very hard, and Kirby
knows it."

Susie Bowman must be some women, I thought. I just
couldn't picture her mentally. She certainly had two sides to her,
feminine and masculine. And then I remembered talking to a
Denver doctor who said some women at birth had a big chunk of
man in them, that actually they should have been born as men,
but by an accident of birth they were given women's bodies.
Susie Bowman must be that kind of woman.

We rode down a long slope to Maroon Creek and crossed
it, a wide stream bed with only a trickle of red water running
through it. Chip pointed upstream to a grove of cottonwoods
that shadowed a small ranch house, a log barn, and several pole
corrals. Not an impressive spread at all, and that surprised me,
Ike Kirby being the kind of man he was.

"Funny fellow, this Kirby," Chip said. "He owns half a
dozen ranches, all of 'em in Wyoming and Utah except Hatchet
yonder. He raised horses here mostly, and keeps only three or
four men. He bought it several years ago after his holdings in
Utah grew to the place where he had to have more range than he
had. It's too high for good winter graze.

"He don't want to ship from Canby because he sells in
Omaha, and it's a direct line from Rawlins on east, so he drives

up there. I think he figured that Hatchet would give him the winter graze he needed, but hell, he found out the winters there are as bad as they are in Utah. That's why he's working to get into the Cove."

He wasn't the first cowman, I thought, who had maneuvered to get the range he wanted. The difference was that most cowmen who had the kind of greed and conscience he did had died years ago. I didn't doubt that the sheriff was his man, probably elected by Kirby's corrupt influence, but what about Oscar Wirt?

"I can't figure this," I said. "I was impressed by Wirt and I can't see him in the light of being Kirby's man, but he goes along with him, doesn't he?"

"Yeah, but only because all the cattlemen in Tremont County who have sizable spreads have similar interests," Chip answered. "It's hard to draw a line here, but I don't believe Wirt would stoop to the kind of tactics Kirby uses. He wants to convict Susie, all right, figuring that if she didn't steal the heifer they arrested her for, she's stolen plenty of others. She has but, damn it, she didn't steal that one."

I didn't know much more than I had before. Obviously Wirt wanted to make an example of Susie, but he surely thought that the hide found on the fence was a plant. If he did, then he was guilty of aiding and abetting a miscarriage of justice, just as much as Kirby was.

I wasn't sure what I'd do or feel if I was in Wirt's boots, but I had to admit that if Susie was a thorn in the side of the big cowmen, maybe I'd try to get rid of her any way I could. But if I did, I wouldn't do it from a judge's position. So I wound up where I'd started; Wirt was a disgrace to the high judicial position he occupied and should be disqualified from hearing Susie's case.

Chapter IX

We rode up a long slope above Maroon creek, then the country leveled off for another five miles. After that we climbed a steep ridge, aiming for a notch in the line of hills ahead. When we rode through it, we pulled up to let our horses blow, and I had my first view of Smith's Cove.

My immediate impression was one of sheer beauty. The valley was two or three miles wide in most places, and five or six long. The Blue River made a streak of silver below us, taking an almost straight east-west course, with a high cliff on the south that rose sheer above the water for five hundred feet or more. To our left the river apparently disappeared into the cliff, making an almost perfect ninety-degree turn.

I pointed to it. "Looks like the river goes down a gopher hole."

"It almost does," Chip said. "You can't see it from here, but it goes into the Canyon of Sorrows, narrow with a lot of rapids and falls. The water churns through there like a millrace. It's a challenge to river runners, and I've never known one who started from this end and came out alive on the other end."

I turned to look west. Timber came down from the hills at the far end of the Cove so it made a dark mass that closed in on the river. From here it looked as if the sheer cliff on the south tapered off into nothing more than a sharp slope. Between here and the edge of the timber was the tillable land, all on the north side of the Blue.

I counted a dozen or more sets of buildings scattered along the north bank. The timbered hills above them knifed down almost to the water in a couple of places, enclosing narrow valleys that drained into the river. I could see what appeared to be a schoolhouse about a mile from where the steep road to our left descended to the level land of the Cove.

"Is that all the settlement there is?" I asked, pointing to the schoolhouse.

Chip nodded. "The store and post office is just across the road." He pointed to a two-story house shaded by several large cottonwoods directly below us. "That's the Bowman place. Alec was the first settler in the Cove, so he located where he wanted. There's a good spring that trickles from the side of the hill above the house, that gives them running water the year around."

The house and outbuildings looked substantial. Most of the other houses were partially hidden by trees, or were too far away for me to see them well enough to determine what they were like, but I had a feeling that the Bowman house was the finest place in the Cove—an assumption I later found to be correct. A number of green patches, probably alfalfa, dotted the Cove, making a sharp contrast to the sage-green of most of the valley floor.

"I suppose people live up those side canyons?" I said.

"A few," Chip said. "Nobody down there is rich and nobody starves to death. Old-man Frisbee has the store and the post office. He's a sort of preacher who marries and buries folks without having any authority to do either, but nobody questions his right to take over. We haven't had a preacher come here from town for five years. Frisbee is a kind of doctor, too. He takes care of everything but injuries and sicknesses that look like they'll be fatal. We have dances in the big room over the store and church in the schoolhouse."

"A self-sufficient community," I said.

"Just about," Chip said. "We have mail which comes out from Canby three times a week. Most folks make the trip to town in the spring and the fall to buy clothes and groceries like salt and sugar. Another thing, Bob. Since I moved to town, I've noticed that folks are happier down here in the Cove than the ones in Canby. Mostly they just want to be let alone. I guess that's the reason they hate Kirby like they do. Life will never be the same if he sends a herd of cattle and a crew of cowboys in here for the winter. We'll have fighting and killing and drinking, and all the Goddamned things people do that make them unhappy." He jerked his head toward the road. "Let's ride down and see if we can find Susie."

"I'm interested in Janey, too," I said. "You told me she was the cook."

"And a damned good one," he said. "We won't have no trouble finding her. She's always on hand. It's Susie who's likely to be anywhere. It's a funny thing about those two women. Nobody ever goes to see Janey. It's always Susie. I guess Janey is sort of like a piece of furniture. She's just there, and it's too bad."

Halfway down the slope the walls on both sides of the road closed in so there was hardly room for two men to ride abreast. Chip called my attention to it. He said, "This is where we stop Kirby if it comes to that. We've got boulders piled up on both sides. All we've got to do is roll 'em onto the road to block it, and Kirby's got a bunch of steers locked up. They can't go on, and it'll be a hell of a job turning 'em back up out of the canyon. Meanwhile it'll be like shooting fish in a barrel to wipe 'em out."

When we reached the bottom, I was aware of how much warmer it was here below in the Cove than it had been on top. I remarked about it. Chip nodded. "It's a son of a bitch down here later in the summer, but everything grows. Janey raises a garden that feeds 'em all winter, and it's never cold like it is in Canby, for instance, so it averages out."

The Bowman house was directly ahead of us, and it was, as it had appeared from the rim, a very substantial building with a wide porch that ran across the front. It was painted white with green trim. When we reined up in front and dismounted, I looked at the window in the front door and noticed a border of colored glass panes that encircled the window. I had seen many front doors like this one, but usually it was a symbol of affluence in the homes of wealthy people. The thought prompted me to ask if Alec Bowman had been a rich man.

"Tolerable," Chip answered. "Rich enough to build the kind of house for his wife that he wanted. It cost him a pile, too, freighting everything in when there wasn't a railroad into Canby."

The lawn was surrounded by a white board fence, the grass was green and trimmed, and behind and to one side of the house I saw the best garden I had ever seen in my life. All of this, I thought, was a tribute to Janey.

The front door was open. Chip led the way into the living room, calling, "Janey!"

She ran out of the kitchen, paused, saw who it was, and let

54

out a whoop. "It's Chip," she cried. "Why didn't you let us know you were coming?"

"Didn't know it till this morning," Chip said, and gathered her into his arms and kissed her.

She clung to him for a moment, saying, "It's been so long since you've been home and you never write."

"Oh, you know I can't write," Chip said, grinning. He motioned to me. "Janey, I want you to meet Bob Norberg. He's a reporter on the *Denver Chronicle*. He wants to stay here for a while."

She turned to me, smiling uncertainly. She was, I thought, a very pretty young woman. Not big, but not small, either, five feet three or four inches, and I doubt that she'd weigh more than one hundred and ten pounds. She had beautiful dark blue eyes, yellow-gold hair, a full-lipped mouth, and a snub nose that was more cute than pretty, but to me it was a distinct asset, marring what would otherwise have been a too-near-perfect face.

She extended a hand, saying, "I'm pleased to meet you, Mr. Norberg. But you know, we're common ranch people, sort of backwoodsy, I guess."

"No, you're not," I said, taking her hand. "You're anything but common. What I want is a chance to work to pay for my room and board."

She withdrew her hand, her gaze on my face, then dropping the full length of my body. She said, "I don't want you to think you're not welcome, but I don't see what we'd have to offer a big-city newspaper man. As for work, that's up to my sister Susie. I attend to the house and she does the outside work."

She was aware, I was sure, that I was wearing a gun, that I had cowboy's clothes on but not the appearance of a cowboy, and she was filled with doubts. "I'm a little soft," I said, "but I've done ranch work. I can hold up my end if we don't start too fast."

"He wants to write about Susie," Chip said, grinning maliciously and knowing he shouldn't have said it just then.

"And you," I added.

"Oh, that's crazy," she said, suddenly flustered. "There's nothing about me that's worth writing about. Susie's the interesting one. Chip, go put your horses away. I'll make some lemonade and you can come back to the house and wait till Susie comes in. She's irrigating the east field, but she ought to be done before long."

"We'll do that," Chip said. "I won't be here very long. I just wanted to be sure Bob got out here without getting his head blowed off. Ike Kirby don't like him much."

"Oh, my," Janey said. "He's a bad one to have not liking you, Mr. Norberg. If you're not on Kirby's side, you must be on ours."

"I am," I said quickly. "That's why my boss sent me out here. There are several things I can't sort out. If I stay here a while, maybe I can."

I turned and followed Chip out of the house, Janey standing motionless and watching us. She was puzzled, I thought. We took care of the horses, took a long drink out of a pipe that fed into the log horse-trough near the barn, and washed up. Chip said, "She'd have fixed us something to eat, but I figured we could stand it till supper. I didn't want to give her too much to do. She'll cook us a big meal. You'll see."

"I like her," I said, "but she's been overlooked all her life. It's done something to her."

Chip nodded agreement. "I ain't sure it's ever bothered her, or whether she ever thought about it. You may find this hard to understand, but she's a hell of a lot happier than Susie."

We returned to the house and sat down in a swing on the front porch, the afternoon shade from the big cottonwoods relieving the heat of the afternoon. I could see that Chip had not exaggerated when he'd said it got disagreeably hot later in the summer.

Janey brought us two tall glasses of lemonade. I leaned back in the porch swing, sipping my lemonade and staring across the front lawn and the level patch of sagebrush that ran to the bank of the river with its fringe of willows. Above it the sandstone cliff was a solid wall, shadowed now with the sun swinging over to the west.

Janey had gone into the kitchen, and we could hear the rattling of pans as she started supper. I sensed that she was uneasy about my presence here and that worried me, because I didn't want her to feel that way, but I understood why she was disturbed.

Everyone who lived in Smith's Cove was isolated and removed from the flow of events. It was like an island which, except for the threat of Kirby's invasion, might have been a thousand miles from what we liked to call civilization. To Janey

Bowman, Denver seemed almost as strange a city as one on the moon might have been.

I saw someone—I assumed it was Susie—walk across the hayfield toward the barn, a shovel over her shoulder. She wore men's clothes, a sloppy-looking hat that was pulled down over her eyes, gum boots, and I noticed she walked with the direct, easy stride of a man. Even after she left the shovel leaning against the barn wall and came on toward the house, I could not see her face clearly.

This was the moment I had been waiting for, and I found my pulse beginning to pound, now that the moment of my meeting the legendary Susie Bowman was at hand.

Chapter X

I heard the hum of conversation from the kitchen for a good five minutes before Susie crossed the living room to the porch, calling, "Chip, you old horse thief. You get tired of cleaning up after a barnful of horses?"

"No, I just couldn't live another day without seeing you," he said.

"You're a damned liar," she said amiably.

"Will you marry me tomorrow?" he asked.

"Hell, no," she answered.

I assumed that this was their usual warm and polite greeting. Having got it over with, she put her arms around him and hugged and kissed him the way a woman would who was in love. At that moment there was nothing masculine about her.

A moment later she released him and turned to me, giving me my first good look at her. She was a big woman, but not grossly big and certainly not fat, just with the big frame and hard body that should have belonged to a man. Still, my first impression of her was that she was very attractive, completely dispelling the mental picture that I'd held of her. This seemed contradictory but, oddly enough, the muscle that hard work had given her did not detract from the feminine quality she possessed.

Susie had taken off her gum boots and put on high-heeled cowboy boots. She still wore the man's shirt and pants I had seen when she'd walked across the barnyard to the kitchen door. Her hair was so dark it was almost black, her eyes were dark brown, and her face was as bronzed by wind and sun as any cowboy's I had ever seen. I liked her—mostly, I think, because I felt an openness, an honesty about her that was unusual and refreshing.

There was this strained moment when we stood facing each other as we made our appraisals, then Chip, who was taking a perverse kind of pleasure out of our meeting, said, "Susie, I want you to meet Bob Norberg. He's a reporter from the *Denver Chronicle*. He's a great admirer of yours."

"The hell!" she said, as if surprised that anyone could admire her, then held out a hand reluctantly as though not really wanting to shake hands, adding, "Janey tells me you want a job working for us."

"That's right," I said, finding her hand as callused as any male farmer's. "I've been assigned the task of writing about your upcoming trial and the situation in Tremont County. I thought the best way to learn what's going on would be to work for you, and also to meet the other people who live in Smith's Cove. It strikes me that everyone here is involved."

She was still studying me as she withdrew her hand and stepped back, her dark eyes continuing to appraise me as coldly as if I were a horse she was interested in buying.

"We don't have a job for you, Mr. Norberg," she said, "and I don't give a damn what your newspaper says either way. We'll stomp our own snakes and we'll do it our way, and I don't need the help of a soft-handed city dude. In the morning you can fork your horse and light out for town."

She didn't sound angry. I should have been furious, but I'd been warned enough about her and what she might do so that I wasn't sore, although what she said was insulting enough. Somehow I had a feeling she hadn't intended to be personal, that she was stating a simple fact.

"Come on, Chip," she said as she turned to him. "It's been a hell of a hot day and I'm dirty. Let's take a swim."

Chip's grin had faded. His expression was sour, as if he hadn't expected that kind of talk to me, even knowing her as well as he did. "Why, Susie," he said, "we can't do that. I didn't bring my suit."

"When did we get so modest we need suits?" she demanded. "Come on."

She grabbed his hand and led him across the yard and on toward the river. I stood motionless as I watched them, thinking that Susie Bowman was indeed an unusual woman. I wondered how many men besides Chip had fallen in love with her, men she had refused to marry. Then I wondered why she had refused them. At least Chip would have made her a good husband, and it was evident that she was fond of him.

I didn't know that Janey had come out of the house to stand beside me until I heard her ask, "What do you think of my plain-spoken sister, Mr. Norberg?"

I turned to see that she was staring at Chip's and Susie's receding backs. When she turned to look at me, I sensed that she was angry, and yet I had a feeling that Susie's reaction to my request was just about what Janey had expected.

"Well, she's an interesting woman," I answered. "I've heard so much about her that I'm not surprised at her saying what she did."

"I am," Janey said tartly. "Mr. Norberg, I've grown up with her and I've lived with her all of my life except for the months when she was in school back East, and I am still surprised at what she says and does." She paused and looked away, biting her lower lip, then she added, "The truth is she should have been born with a man's body. Our father wanted a son. Susie's the nearest thing he got to one."

"Yet she seems very much a woman," I said.

"Oh, she is," Janey said quickly. "If you stayed here, you'd be surprised at how much of a woman she is."

"I'm sorry about the way she feels," I said. "I think I could do something for her. From what I hear, she'll be convicted at her next trial. Judge Wirt will see to it."

"He'll try." Impulsively Janey reached out and laid a hand on my arm. "I'm sorry, too. She could use some help, both here with the ranch work and with her defense. But you will stay with us tonight. Don't let her scare you off. There's a bed upstairs that will not be in use, and you're welcome to use it tonight or even longer if you want to."

As long as I live, I will never forget the compassion I saw on Janey's face, the sympathy of someone who had lived with Susie's stubborn and bullheaded nature and who shared with me the bite of her cutting tongue.

"Thank you," I said, "but I think one night will be enough."

"Susie runs the outside work," Janey said. "I run the house. Susie never argues with me about what I decide as long as it concerns the house and garden, and not the ranch work."

Janey had withdrawn her hand from my arm and now

stepped back, her gaze on the willows where Susie and Chip had disappeared. Suddenly she began to cry. I turned toward her, startled, thinking she had nothing to cry about.

"What's the matter?" I asked.

As soon as the words left my mouth, I knew I was a fool for asking. Whatever the trouble was, it had to be too involved to explain it to a stranger who had known her only a few hours. Stranger or not, she fell into my arms as if she did not have the strength to stand by herself. I hugged her, her face against the front of my shirt, and let her cry. I never professed to know much about women, but I did know that sometimes crying was the best relief they could get from emotional pressure.

I don't know how long it took her to get over her crying jag, but when she did, she tipped her head back and tried to smile, tears still running down her face. "Thank you," she said. "I don't know what got into me. If you're still here tomorrow, I'll tell you what's the matter. I can't do it now."

I don't know to this day whether she wanted to be kissed or not, but she didn't move for several seconds, her face upturned to mine, her full, red lips slightly parted. I felt a hunger in her, a compelling desire to be loved, and as crazy as it sounds for the short time I had known her, I knew I wanted to love her and I wanted her to love me—Bob Norberg, a man who had known many women, but had never met one who could be taken seriously. In fact, I had been burned twice by women I thought loved me. Anyhow, I kissed her, and a kiss that was intended to be a brotherly peck of comfort turned out to be the longest and most sensuous kiss I had ever experienced.

Suddenly she jerked away, her face turning scarlet. "Oh, what happened to me? I'm sorry. I don't know what you'll think of me."

She whirled and ran through the living room and on into the kitchen. Several startling things had happened in the last few minutes, but the way she whirled and ran was the most startling. I followed, saying, "I think you're..."

"Don't say it," she cried. "Go back and sit down on the porch and don't bother me. I've got to get supper."

I hesitated a moment, staring at her back as she stoked up the fire, then I turned and walked back to the porch, knowing I had better take her at her word. Women!, I thought in disgust as I sat down in the swing. Then it occurred to me that I had no right to be critical of Janey. She had turned to me simply because I was handy; there had to be something very deep between her and Susie that had to be settled between them sometime. There was nothing an outsider could do.

Time passed slowly. I could hear Janey bustling around in the kitchen, I smelled meat frying, and I was hungry enough to eat the steak raw, but there was nothing I could do but sit there and wait. Presently, the sun seemingly so low in the west that it touched the line of hills, Chip and Susie came through the willows and approached the house, their hair wet, both smiling as they walked toward me holding hands.

As I watched them, it seemed to me that they were unquestionably in love. Susie needed Chip's help to run the ranch. There was no reason that I could see why they shouldn't get married, no reason except that Susie wouldn't marry him. That, I told myself, made her the worst kind of fool. Again I had to remind myself that no man understands a woman, and I was the fool for trying to judge her—Susie Bowman of all women.

Janey appeared in the door and shouted, "Come and get it before I throw it out."

Susie said something to Chip and they began to run.

Chapter XI

Supper was a strange meal. Not that the food wasn't good. On the contrary, it was excellent: steak fried perfectly, fluffy mashed potatoes, green peas from Janey's garden, biscuits that practically melted in my mouth, sweet golden butter, honey, coffee, and lemon pie for dessert. Sure, I was abnormally hungry, but still it was one of the best meals I'd ever eaten. Janey was as good a cook as Chip had said.

No, the strange quality came from our relationship at the table. Janey didn't say a word unless she was asked a question, and there weren't many of those. She sat with her eyes on her plate, except when she rose to bring the coffee pot to the table or the pie from the pantry. I felt guilty because I had kissed her. I knew it made her feel guilty and that in turn made her miserable.

Chip and Susie made the situation worse by their conversation, which was strictly with each other. My chair might just as well have been empty. Most of the talk was about the people who lived in Smith's Cove. Chip had not been here for a long time and apparently had little if any correspondence with either Susie or Janey.

Of course I knew none of these people, so I had nothing to say even if I'd wanted to, but I was irritated by what seemed to me unnecessary rudeness. Even if Susie didn't like me and was sending me packing in the morning, I was an overnight guest and ordinary courtesy would have dictated that at least some of the conversation be directed at me.

I grew angry and then just plain mad. By now I was convinced that I was being ignored for a purpose—to convince me I'd better leave in the morning no matter what Janey had said to me or how I felt.

When we'd finished our pie and the last cup of coffee, Susie leaned back in her chair and rolled a cigarette. On occasion I had seen women smoke, but not a so-called "good woman," and I guess it bothered me. As she sealed her cigarette and slipped it into her mouth, I said, "Miss Bowman, you made it plain that you aim to stomp your own snakes. Just how do you figure to stomp Judge Wirt?"

She was startled, I guess. Maybe she had thought the chilly treatment she had given me would freeze my tongue. She took the cold cigarette out of her mouth and stared at me a moment, resentfully, I thought, then she said sharply, "That's my business, mister."

"Then you're accepting a sure guilty verdict," I said, "and you'll willingly go to the pen?"

"Why, Goddamn you," she sputtered, "I'm not doing anything of the kind. What makes you so smart about what's going to happen to me?"

"I spent enough time in Canby to hear a few things," I said. "Even with Chip's testimony, which is considered suspect, you'll be found guilty. Judge Wirt will instruct the jury in such a way that you won't have a chance. He makes no bones about his feelings that you should have been found guilty, and that a second trial is a waste of taxpayers' money."

Susie shrugged "I'm not worried about Judge Wirt's instructions to the jury. I may not be found innocent, but I'll get another hung jury and the county won't go through the expense of a third trial."

"Another thing I've wondered about is your choice of attorney," I said. "I talked to Fred Pherson. I don't think he gave you adequate representation during your trial."

"For once you're right, Mr. Reporter," she said. "He won't be my lawyer next time." She struck a match, fired her cigarette, and shook the match flame out. "Now if you're done retrying my case for me, I'll go out on the porch where it's cooler."

She rose and left the kitchen, Chip following after he glanced uneasily at me. I looked at Janey, who was staring after them, a worried expression on her face. I said, "Janey, I want to finish what I started to say before supper. You wouldn't let me finish then, but..."

"Don't finish it now," she said as she jumped up. "I couldn't stand to hear it. About Susie, Mr. Norberg. I think you're wasting your time trying to help her. Sometimes I feel she wants to be found guilty. She acts like a person bent on committing suicide."

I hadn't thought of it that way. I sat staring at Janey, wondering if she was right, and why. She rose and started clearing the table. I said, "I'll help you with the dishes."

"No, you won't," she said. "Housework is my job. I don't shove it off on anyone else. You go out to the porch where it's cooler."

Irritated, I walked out of the kitchen, wondering if I'd ever get a chance to tell her how much I respected and liked her. She was mixed up on a lot of things, I thought, finding in her housework the reason for living, and thereby gaining an equality of sorts with Susie. I wondered what sort of man Alec Bowman had been, if he had spoiled Susie because she was like a son to him, and had abused Janey.

I joined Chip and Susie on the porch and sat down with my back to a post. They were in the swing holding hands and talking, completely ignoring me which was what I had expected. The twilight was close to complete darkness, the cliff across the river a faint line against the sky. As I glanced at it, the thought struck me that the cliff was a symbol of the Cove people: tough, independent, and hard enough to stand against any pressure that could be brought against then. Obviously it had stood there for a very long time.

Suddenly I was aware that something or someone was moving out there on the other side of the road. At first I thought it was an animal, a loose horse or cow. The light was so thin I couldn't be sure of what I was seeing, but as I watched it move along the edge of the brush, I decided it was a man on a horse. Then it stopped and I lost it.

"Excuse me for interrupting you," I said, "but somebody is out there who doesn't want us to know he's there."

"Oh, hell," Susie said impatiently, "you city men are afraid of your shadows. Being out here in the wilderness is making you boogery."

"Bob don't get boogery at nothing," Chip said and rose. "Somebody tried to kill him when he was asleep in his hotel room in Canby. The killer may have followed him out here."

"I'll be damned," Susie said. "So you really got shot at?

65

What'd you do, crawl under the bed?"

"Susie, sometimes you are downright impossible," Chip said angrily. "Bob chased him out of the hotel, but he got away. Our efficient sheriff sat on his butt and didn't do anything, which is what I'd expect him to do."

Susie rose and came toward me, peering at me in the near darkness. She asked, "Are you giving it to me straight, or is this your usual newspaper bull?"

"No bull," I said, trying to hold my anger down. The woman was, as Chip had said, impossible. "It's one reason I'm here. Not long before I left Denver three men, including Kirby, met with a man named Van Tatum in a hotel room. Tatum has never been convicted of murder, but he is a known assassin. He was in Canby this morning renting a horse from Chip. He's going by the name of Vic Tate."

She gripped my arm and shook it, her voice edged by fear. "Are you trying to tell me he's the man out there waiting to take a shot at you?"

"Or you," I said.

"Me? Why me?"

"I think Tatum was sent here to murder somebody," I said. "At the time he was in the meeting in Denver, no one except my boss knew I was coming to Canby, so I couldn't be the target. I think he made the decision himself to kill me. The question is, who else is here in Smith's Cove that Kirby wants killed besides you?"

"Let's get inside," Chip said. "We can't see the bastard. He might be sneaking up on us."

Susie didn't argue. She led the way into the house and shut the door. A lighted lamp was on the stand in the middle of the room. I started to say she'd better blow the lamp out when Susie asked, "Who else was in that meeting besides Kirby?"

"Judge Wirt," I said. "The third man was not identified."

Susie was visibly shocked when I mentioned Wirt's name. I'd had a feeling that she thought she'd received a fair trial from Wirt and that she would again. Now the thought that he might have sent Tatum here to kill her was more than she could accept, and she began to shake her head.

"You're lying," Susie said. "Or somebody is. Why would Kirby or the Judge want me murdered?"

I had crossed to the stand, deciding I'd blow the lamp out myself. I glanced at the window near the door and froze. A face

66

was plastered against the glass. Van Tatum! I couldn't mistake that face. It was unquestionably the man I'd seen in the livery stable.

The instant Tatum realized I was looking at him, he jerked away from the window. I blew the lamp out, yelled, "Get down," and lunged toward the door, jerked it open, and went on through it to the porch. I heard the pound of feet as Tatum raced away from the house. I fired at the sound, and knew immediately I had wasted a bullet.

I moved to one side, my cocked gun in my hand, eyes probing the darkness, but I couldn't make out any trace of movement. Night had settled down. I could see nothing except the blackness of the cliff across the river, so I had no idea where he had gone or what he would do now. A prickle raced down my spine. A man who could move as swiftly and silently through the darkness might be circling back this very second. If I hadn't seen him, he would probably have fired through the window, and one or more of us would be dead.

I waited, eyes straining, head cocked to listen. Chip joined me, asking, "Think he's still around?"

"I don't know," I said.

A moment later we heard the pound of hoofs, then a couple of shots as he fired at us, more in defiance, I thought, than with the idea of hitting anyone. Both Chip and I shot at the flashes of gunflame, and when their echoes had died, we heard briefly the fading beat of hoofs and then the sound was gone.

We returned to the living room and I lit the lamp. Susie was standing in the middle of the room looking dazed. Janey had come out of the kitchen and stood staring at us, obviously shocked by the sudden eruption of violence. Chip pulled the blinds and closed the door. He said, "We'll bar the doors, Susie. He's probably gone for good, but let's not give him any chance of coming back and slipping into the house. If he breaks in through a window, we'll hear him."

I'm not sure Susie heard. She was looking at me, a strange expression on her face, as if having trouble grasping all that had happened and the implications of these events. She swallowed, the defiance that had been in her from the moment we'd first met now entirely gone.

"I've changed my mind, Bob," she said. "You can go to work for us in the morning."

Chapter XII

A moment of silence followed Susie's statement that I would go to work for her in the morning. I heard Janey take in a long breath. I saw that Chip was looking at Susie in amazement, as if not sure he knew what she was up to. I was surprised, too, so surprised I didn't say anything for a moment.

Chip was the first to recover. "Well, Susie," he said, "I didn't think you were going to come to your senses in time to keep him."

"I'll accept the deal right off," I said, "before you change your mind."

"Oh, she won't change again," Chip said. "It's a miracle she changed it this time."

"Don't be a smart-ass, Chip Malone," she said angrily. "I know I'm bullheaded and stubborn and ornery as a he-goat, but I know what I want and what I don't want. I sure didn't want a nosey Denver reporter digging into our business. I'm not sure how we're going to get along, but I owe you something. If you hadn't seen that bastard when you did, he could have shot us before we made a move. I doubt that you'll do enough work to justify feeding you, but we'll give it a shot."

"My God, Susie," Chip said indignantly, "can't you say anything without turning it into an insult?"

"It's not an insult," she snapped. "I've got to be showed, that's all. I admit I haven't been fair. I condemned him before I knew anything about him. It's just that I don't have any use for city people, and I have less use for newspaper reporters because they're always after something sensational that will gain more readers."

"Maybe you'd better know that my boss is convinced you're being framed and he thought we could help," I said. "That's why I'm here—along with the fact that he knew your mother years ago and is interested in the welfare of her daughters."

I suspected they knew nothing of Sid Gorman's interest in their mother and I had no intention of giving them the details, but it irked me to hear Susie run down newspapers and reporters as if they were all the same. I thought telling them might make a difference in how they felt, but I could see it meant nothing to Susie.

"That's nice," she said, dismissing the matter as of no importance. "Now maybe you'll tell me why you think Kirby and Wirt or anybody else wants me killed."

"I don't believe it's Wirt," I said, "even though he was at the meeting I told you about. I think he wants to send you to the pen as an example of what happens to small-time rustlers. He says it isn't big in individual cases, but add it all up and it becomes a big loss in the county. It's different with Kirby. He may have given different orders to Tatum than Wirt did, but he considers you the leader of the Cove people, and he'd get his winter range without any trouble if you were out of the way."

She thought about that a minute, then nodded. "Since he failed tonight, he'll try again."

"Maybe," I said. "You can't outguess that kind of man. He may still be trying for me. After talking to Wirt, I think the ones they're really after are the so-called known rustlers. Wirt may believe in law and order and talk about it from the bench, but he knows the sheriff will never bring these men in, and he's had all the rustling in this county he can stomach."

"Ash Morck and Ned Rusk are the ones they call 'known rustlers'," Susie said. "They've lived here for several years and nobody knows for sure. All we really know is that they disappear for weeks, then show up and live here just as if they had been here all the time." She laughed. "If this man Tatum is here to murder them, he's out of luck. They've been gone for a month, and if they operate the way they have in the past, they'll be gone for another two or three weeks."

"Maybe he'll get discouraged and leave," Chip said.

I shook my head. "Not a man like Van Tatum. He's taken

a job and probably been paid half of his fee. He'll stick around until he earns the rest of it."

"I'm tired." Susie took Chip's hand as she turned toward her bedroom. "You want to sleep with me?"

He winked at me as she led him toward her bedroom. "I wouldn't miss it," he said.

Janey sighed. When the door closed, she said, "Now you know what sort of a sister I have. Are you going to put that into your newspaper story?"

"Of course not," I said indignantly. "It's nobody's business but theirs."

She walked to the stand and picked up the lamp. "I'll show you to your room. You're in for some hard work. Susie drives everybody. She rolls out of bed before the sun's up and you'll be doing the same thing if you're going to work for her."

She led the way up the stairs and turned into the first room to her right. She placed the lamp on the bureau as she said, "I hope you'll be comfortable."

The room was plainly furnished with a bed covered by a colorful quilt. I was never an expert on patterns, but I thought this was called the butterfly. There was one straight-backed chair, a pine bureau holding a pitcher and a basin, and a slop jar on the floor beside the bureau. Two pictures were on the wall, oil paintings of Pike's Peak and the Garden of the Gods. The first thing I noticed was that the room was clean. Aside from that, it was little different from the room I'd had in the Canby Hotel.

"It's stuffy in here," Janey said as she opened a window. "I should have come up before supper and opened a window." She turned toward the door, adding, "I'm glad you're staying."

"So am I." I took her by the arm and turned her toward the bed. "Sit down. I've got to talk to you. I won't sleep unless I do."

She tried to jerk free, but I held her arm and forced her to sit on the bed, then I dropped down beside her. I put an arm around her and said, "Now you listen to me, Janey. I admire and respect you. I don't know what's bothering you, but if it has anything to do with me, quit worrying."

She sat stiffly as if frozen, her face turned away from me. I said, "Maybe it has nothing to do with me, maybe I'm just thinking too much of myself. If it is something else, just forget what I said."

"No." She turned to look at me and then began to cry. "I

made such a fool of myself, Bob. Of course it has to do with you. I acted like a wanton. You must despise me."

She had trouble getting the words out between her sobs. I hugged her harder and she pressed against me as if somehow gaining strength from me. I let her cry until the tears stopped coming, then she rose and wiped her eyes, walked across the room to a window and stood looking out into the darkness.

"I don't despise you at all," I said. "I think you're wonderful."

"Do you?" she asked, as if she didn't really believe what I said.

"Of course I do," I said.

She was silent for quite a while. I stayed on the bed looking at her back and not knowing what to say or do, so I just waited. After a time she began to talk, finding relief, I think, in the flow of words.

"You are the first visitor we've had for a long time," she said slowly, "except for Chip, who is part of the family, and the men who come to sleep with Susie. I wanted you to think well of me. There's a big world out there I've never seen, and you are a part of that world. You see, I'm my mother's daughter. Susie was my father's. She tried to act the part of a son. I was raised to keep house, to be refined, to be a lady. Daddy thought it was smart for Susie to act like a boy.

"Mama fought with him about Susie, and when she got expelled from high school in Canby, he finally agreed to send her East to school with the idea that it would turn her into a lady. That was Mama's idea. Daddy said it couldn't be done and he actually didn't want her to be a lady, but he gave in to Mama. It didn't work, just like he knew it wouldn't. Susie broke every rule the school had, so they finally wrote to Daddy to come and get her.

"Mama died when I was fifteen. Since then I've been a housekeeper. Susie worked outside with Daddy until he died from a heart attack three years ago. She's kept the ranch going since then, and she's taken Daddy's place as a community leader. People in the Cove like her and look up to her and they'll follow her, even though they gossip about her morals. Ike Kirby is right if he thinks when she's dead he'll have no trouble moving his herd into the Cove. The opposition to him would be totally disorganized without Susie's leadership."

She turned to face me. "I guess all of this has nothing to do with what you'll write for your paper, but it may explain some things to you. Susie lives her own life. Half of the men in the Cove have slept with her and, for some crazy reason I don't understand, the wives don't say anything. She lusts for men like most men lust for women. I can't be that way. I want one man. I want to marry him and have children. Susie doesn't. She says she needs more than one man."

"Is that why she won't marry Chip?"

Janey nodded. "I think she loves him, and not just as a brother as she keeps saying, but I don't think she'll ever marry him. So someday he'll leave the country and never come back. She'll be sorry then. I know she will."

She paused, looking at me as if wanting to say something more, then she went on slowly, picking each word carefully, "I have quit apologizing for what Susie does. She has always done exactly what she wanted to and I guess she always will. You'll just have to get used to being around a woman like that. I think most men are like her, and maybe she acts the way she does because she tries to be like a man. Well, I'd better let you go to bed. It will be a short night for you."

She walked to the door, paused long enough to say, "Good night, Bob," and left the room.

I went to bed, but I found it hard to sleep. I kept thinking about Janey saying it was a big world out there that she had never seen, that I was the first visitor they'd had for a long time. In a way she was a slave and not her own person, caught here by a sense of family duty and lack of money, that would have given her freedom. I felt sorry for her, but most of all I knew I liked her very much.

Chapter XIII

Janey was right. Susie worked the tail off me. I had never worked so hard for my father. My muscles, soft from city living, hardened up after the first week, so I was able to keep up with Susie and not feel when I got out of bed in the morning that every joint and muscle in my body was screaming with pain.

Chip stayed for a week and I think he saved me. He knew I needed time, so he found ways to slow things up for a few minutes so I could get my wind, but if Susie ever gave me a thought, she never showed it. She seemed downright sadistic. I'm convinced she thought I would give up and leave, proving what she'd thought all the time—that city men were cream puffs. But after I'd stuck it out for a week, and didn't complain or say a word about going back to Denver, I think she began to have some respect for me.

We irrigated. It was hard and dirty and tiring and I hated it. I didn't mind the branding, and again it was Chip who saved the day for me. He stayed until we had finished and had driven the cattle back into the hills to the north, where the grass was green and lush. I'm sure the range could have stood more cattle than were being run on it, but the Cove people were right in contending that it wouldn't hold up if Kirby's herd was thrown in along with the Cove cattle.

The morning Chip left he kissed Susie. It was more or less perfunctory, it seemed to me. He had slept with her every night since we'd come, but I had a hunch that the first flame of passion had been burned off for Susie. She wasn't really upset about his leaving, but she went through the routine of kissing and hugging him and making him promise to come back as soon as he could get another week off.

He held her at arm's length for a few seconds just staring at her, the corners of his mouth working. I thought he was going to break down, and maybe he would have if Susie had been more responsive. It was clear enough that he hated to leave, that he was haunted by the feeling he would never see her again, but I don't think she sensed that at all.

When he turned to Janey it was different. She ran into his arms and kissed him with an ardor Susie had not even hinted at. Then she just hugged him and cried for a minute or two. When she finally stepped back and wiped her eyes, she said, "Chip Malone, if you don't write to us and tell us how you're getting along, I'm going to ride into Canby and find out for myself."

He patted her on the back. "I'll write," he said. "I promise."

He shot a glance at Susie as if wanting to tell her he might never be back, but he didn't say anything as he turned toward the door.

"Don't forget," Janey said. "You're a part of the family. You remember that."

"I'll remember," he said and jerked his head at me. "Come on, Bob. Let's go saddle my horse."

I followed him outside, knowing he wanted to say something to me without Susie being there to hear. Ordinarily she would have gone out with us, but apparently she caught his meaning and stayed with Janey. The way she usually ran over people I was surprised she stayed in the house, so I was forced to admit she was a little more sensitive than I thought she was.

Chip didn't say anything all the way to the corral. I didn't know what to say, but when we reached the corral, I asked, "Is she going to marry you?" I'll never know why I asked, and I knew immediately it had been the wrong thing to say. As soon as the words were out of my mouth, I wished I could have pulled them back, but I guess nobody has learned to do that.

Chip scowled as he took his rope off a corral post. He started to open the gate, then stopped and looked at me. "You know damned well she ain't," he said sourly. "She needed me the first three or four nights we were here, then she was satisfied. If I stayed another night, I'd be sleeping with you."

He slapped the rope against his thigh a few times and stood staring at the cliff across the river. "Maybe all women are the same, but I don't believe it. If I'd fallen in love with Janey, everything would have been fine. But hell no, it had to be Susie. I don't know why unless it was the challenge. I've known ever since I was little how she is, which same makes me the world's biggest fool."

"It's happened to a lot of men," I said.

"Janey likes you," he said. "She's a sister to me and a hell of a good one. She deserves a man, a good one. I hope it turns out to be you."

"So do I," I said. "She's not like any other woman I've ever met."

"I'm going to ask you to do something," Chip said. "If you don't feel like doing it, just say so. I know it's an imposition, but it might turn out to be something you can use. I'm going to Hicks in a few days. I'm not sure just when. I'll talk to my boss and when he finds somebody to work for him, I'll take off. I don't think I'll ever come back here. It hurts too damned much."

I nodded. "I can understand that."

"I don't know what will happen to Susie," he said. "She's so damned stubborn, but maybe she can't help herself. She's not a happy person, but she sure brings her unhappiness on herself. Well, what I wanted to ask was if you'd ride up to Hicks when I go? I've told you about Al Galt, the Hicks marshal. I know he's Kirby's man, and Kirby wants me dead to keep me from testifying at Susie's trial. The man I've got to see lives in Hicks, so I have to stop there. Galt will find a way to gun me down if he can. I'd like for you to be there to back me up. He might hold off if he knows who you are."

"Sure, I'll go," I said, "but don't forget that Kirby wants me dead, too."

He frowned. "I hadn't thought of that. Maybe you'd better not go."

"No, I want to," I said quickly, "but when we're in town, we'd better stick together."

"If you think Kirby might..."

"No," I interrupted. "Just let me know when you're going and I'll ride into town. If Kirby really wants to rub me out, he'll get the job done right here."

"I suppose so," Chip said. "Maybe Galt won't know anything about you. Kirby wouldn't expect you to show up in Hicks."

He opened the corral gate, went in, and roped and saddled

his horse, then led him out of the corral. He held his hand out, trying to grin, but it turned into more of a grimace than a grin. He said, "I think you're gonna make it with Susie. Drop me a line if anything comes up I ought to know."

I shook hands, sensing the longing that was in the man. He wanted to make his home here, to be a part of the Bowman family, to have Susie for a wife, but he was a realist and he knew very well it would never happen.

"I will," I promised. "I'm sure you're right about me being able to use whatever happens while you're in Hicks."

He stepped into the saddle, lifted a hand in salute, and rode away. I watched him go, noting that he looked at the house until he was past it. Then he put his horse into a gallop and disappeared into the narrow canyon that held the road which led out of Smith's Cove.

I had a lump in my throat. He was a hell of a good man, too good to spend his life cleaning out a livery stable, but he stayed in Canby to be close to Susie and be on hand to testify at her trial. Now he had reached an emotional crisis that was forcing him to leave, but he would still be close enough to get to the trial when it was held, and close enough to get back here in a hurry if Susie changed her mind about marrying him.

I didn't know that Susie had left the house until she said, "He left finally, did he? I thought you never were going to get done talking."

I was irritated by the casual way she had let Chip go, and I guess I snapped at her, "Why don't you marry him? He loves you so much he's sick because he has to leave."

She started toward the barn, then she swung around and glared at me. "Let me set a rule down right now, Mr. Reporter. I answer to no man. Who I marry or who I don't marry, and why I do or don't, is none of your Goddamned business."

I was out of line and I knew it. For a moment I was afraid I was going to lose my chance of staying here, so I said quickly, "I'm sorry. You're dead right. It's just that I like Chip..."

"So do I," she said, mollified by my apology. "Don't misunderstand me. I like Chip better than any other man I know, but I'm not the marrying kind. When I'm older maybe I'll change, but now I need variety."

She was trying to act like a man again, I thought. I considered telling her that Chip was taking a job near Hicks, and there was a good chance he'd get killed before he left town, but I didn't. If she wanted to be let alone, I'd sure as hell better do it.

"Well, boss," I said, "what are we going to do today?"

"We're going to start getting in our winter's supply of wood," she said. "We've got to move the wood rack onto the wagon, then we'll harness up and start out. We'll be gone all day, so I had Janey pack a lunch for us."

We were on our way in less than half an hour, heading straight up the slope toward the timber—a saw, a double-bitted ax, a sledge, and a couple of wedges in the wagon. We reached the timber but Susie kept on, twisting through the trees until we came to a dead one.

"I'm not going to cut any live trees until I have to," she said. "It takes God a long time to grow a tree, but man can cut one down in fifteen minutes."

I had never used a crosscut saw and I hadn't done much with an ax, so my performance was poor, to say the least, but Susie, bless her, ignored my ineptness. I soon found I could split the logs more effectively than I could saw, so I used the sledge and wedge. By five o'clock we had worked up enough wood in four-foot lengths to fill the rack, so we quit.

While we were unloading behind the house, I said, "I haven't sent anything to the paper since I got here. If I don't get something in the mail, I'll get fired. I'd like to ride to the post office tonight and mail what I've written."

"I'll go with you," she said. "We need some things from the store. Besides, there might be a few questions you want to ask old-man Frisbee. He wouldn't give you an answer about the weather if you went alone."

"What questions did you have in mind?"

"For one thing, I'd like to know if this bastard Tatum has showed his face around the store."

"I'd thought about that and had wondered if he had," I said.

"He's let us alone since that first night," she said. "What do you make of that?"

"I think he's back in the hills waiting for Ash Morck and Ned Rusk to show up," I answered. "Once he gets that done, we may hear from him again."

"How about going after him?" she said.

"If the work isn't crowding us, it might be a good idea," I said.

"I'm not very brave when it comes to getting shot at from

the brush," she said, "but shooting it out with him is different. I've got to admit I've been scared ever since he took those shots at us."

"So have I," I said. "We'd better have a talk with Frisbee. If he's seen Tatum, we'll know he's still in the country."

"I'll tell Janey we'll be late for supper," she said.

Fifteen minutes later we were headed for the store.

Chapter XIV

The store was empty when we went in. I glanced around, thinking it was more primitive than most country stores I'd seen. There was a bar on one side, just two planks laid across two sawhorses. A dozen or more bottles were on the shelves behind the bar. Groceries were on the other side, but these shelves, too, were less than half filled. At the far end were a couple of shelves that held clothes: work shirts, pants, long-handled underwear, hats, boots, and some dress goods.

I finally spotted the cubbyhole in the back that was the post office, a grilled window with a slot below it and a sign that said MAIL. I slid my envelope through it, wondering if it would ever leave the Cove.

"How often does the mail go out?" I asked.

"Three times a week," she answered. "It goes tomorrow."

"Good," I said. "Susie, it looks to me as if the Cove people go to Canby for what they have to buy."

She nodded agreement. "Say it in a low tone so he can't hear. He gets madder'n hell if he does hear anyone say that." She raised her voice, calling, "Mr. Frisbee."

A moment later he came out of the back room chewing on a sizable quid of tobacco. He peered at us for a moment, then he said as if pleased, "Why, Susan, what brings you here this time of day? You ought to be home eating some of Janey's good cooking."

He was indeed an old man with a white beard and white hair, stoop-shouldered, but with the bright blue eyes of one who shows no sign of senility. I had seen a few old people who appeared to be immortal and he was a good example, possessing a body that was showing the ravages of time, but with a mind as keen as it was the day he was twenty-one.

He looked me over from the crown of my Stetson to the toes of my boots, then he said, "Who is this jayhoo?"

Susie had made no effort to introduce us, but she'd known him a long time. Maybe he had to have his moment of appraisal before he was interested in finding out who I was.

"He's Bob Norberg," Susie said. "He's working for me."

"Hmpf!" Frisbee squinted at me, his gaze moving the length of my body again. "Is he any good?"

"He's learning," she said, an evasive answer that wasn't exactly a commendation. "I'm not paying him any wages. Just his board."

"He don't look like much," Frisbee said. "Chances are that's all he's worth."

"He's also a reporter for the *Denver Chronicle*," Susie said.

"Reporter?" Frisbee shouted the word as if he didn't believe it. "What in blue blazes of hell is he doing in an out-of-the-way, piddling hole in the ground like Smith's Cove?"

I was getting damned tired of standing there and being talked about as if I was a stick of furniture. I said, "I'm looking into Susie's arrest and trial. I'm convinced she was framed, and I don't think the next trial will give her justice."

"Well, now, that's plumb interesting, coming from a big-city reporter." He squinted at me again as if not yet believing I was real, then he pursed his lips and spat in the direction of the nearest spittoon, which was located next to the cracker barrel. "What do you aim to do about it?"

"Find out the truth any way I can, and then print it," I said. "I thought the best way was to spend some time in the Cove and get to know Susie and Janey and talk to people like you who know them. I'm more concerned right now about our safety than I am the trial."

"What does that mean?" he demanded.

"Have any strangers stopped here within the last week or so?" I asked.

"Yeah, there was," Frisbee said. "One tall, dark-complected bird. Looked like he might have been a 'breed. Hell of a mean-looking bastard. We ain't had nobody in the Cove who looked like him since the Wild Bunch used to hang out here, and I don't think any of them looked as low-down mean as this son of a bitch did. He bought some grub and walked out."

"Did he say anything?"

"Not much," Frisbee answered, "except that he was a friend of Ned Rusk and Ash Morck. Wanted to know where they lived."

I looked at Susie and nodded. It pretty well proved that my theory was right. Tatum had come to Smith's Cove to murder these two men. She nodded back, her face grave.

"Well?" Frisbee demanded. "Who is he? What's he here for?"

"His name is Van Tatum," I said. "We think he's here to murder some of the Cove people who are supposed to be rustlers."

"Us, too," Susie said. "He stopped at our place and peeked in a window. Bob saw him and he ran, then he shot at us a couple of times."

Frisbee's weathered old face turned pale. He wiped a hand across his mouth and swallowed. "Damn me! I told him where they lived. If they get plugged, it'll be my doing."

"You didn't know," I said. "I understand that Rusk and Morck are not in the Cove now. Do you know when they'll be back?"

Frisbee shrugged. "Who knows? If they perform like they usually do, I'd say it'll be three weeks or more, but hell, they don't tell nobody where they're going, what they'll be doing, or when they'll be home."

I turned toward the door and walked out, thinking we had learned all we could. Susie said, "Thank you, Mr. Frisbee," and caught up with me. We mounted and rode back toward the Rafter B.

"You want to go after him in the morning?" I asked.

"No," she answered. "I think we'll need Ash and Ned's help. If he's here to kill them, he'll probably let us alone until he does what he was paid to do, so I think we'll be safe until they get back."

"If we know when they get back," I said.

"Frisbee will know," she said. "They'll come to the store for supplies. I'll tell Frisbee to get word to us as soon as he sees them. Oh hell, I forgot the sack of flour Janey wanted."

She didn't say anything more until we reached the corral and off-saddled, then she said, "It's been hotter'n hell today. Let's go for a swim."

It hadn't been that hot, but I hadn't been swimming since I'd been here and the idea appealed to me. She had gone with Chip several times, but I hadn't been invited. I wasn't sure why, because Susie was never deterred from doing what she wanted to by a mere matter of modesty. She didn't know the word.

I hesitated answering her because I was hungry. I said, "We ought to eat supper first. Janey will be expecting us."

"She'll keep supper warm," Susie said. "Come on."

I went with her, more from curiosity than anything else. I wanted to see her naked. She had been an enigma to me from the first. I found it hard to believe she was made like other women, but when we reached the river and she took off her clothes, I saw that she was except that she had a far more beautiful body than most women. Her trim breasts were perfect, her butt as shapely as any I had ever seen. The only difference with other women was the fact that her muscles were developed more than most, but it did not detract from her physical beauty.

She faced me for a moment, a tantalizing half-smile on her lips. She stood tall and straight, her shoulders back, legs slightly spread. She gave me a good look, then she said, "Last one in is a rotten egg," and jumped into the water.

I followed her as she struck out for the other side. She was a far better swimmer than I was. I had never seen a seal in the water, but I was convinced that she would have put the best of them to shame. She crossed to the cliff on the other side, swimming in long, clean strokes, whipped around and passed me before I was within ten feet of the cliff.

She was lying on her back in the warm sand when I reached the bank where we'd started. I lay down beside her wondering why we didn't get our clothes on and go to the house for our supper, but obviously she had other plans. We were silent for a moment, then I was aware of the roar of the river below us in the Canyon of Sorrows.

"If a person forgot where he was and let himself get much farther downstream, he'd be swept into the canyon, wouldn't he?" I asked.

She sat up and turned to face me. "That's right," she said. "It's happened more than once. Their bodies were never found."

She sat with her knees in front of her, arms around them.

Suddenly she dropped her arms and spread her legs, her eyes on me, anticipation in them as she waited to see if I was going to accept her invitation. I didn't, but she saw the effect she had on me and laughed softly.

"You're too good to waste," she said, and before I could move, she was on top of me.

I had never had a woman on top of me, always believing that it was the natural order of things for a man to be on top, and for a moment I thought of trying to shove her off, but I didn't think about it very long. I didn't have time. She was making hard thrusts against me, much as a man would have made if he had been on top.

It was not the time to argue with her. I surrendered myself to the passion of the moment, and it didn't last much longer than a moment. It seemed only a matter of seconds until I exploded, and she was pressing against me as if needing to extract every bit of satisfaction that was possible. I felt her pulsating throb as she clung to me. Presently she relaxed, her face dropping to my chest, her dead weight falling against me. She remained that way for several minutes before she rolled off to lie on her back in the sand beside me.

She took a long breath, turning her head to smile timidly at me, an expression I had never seen on her face before. For a short time I was seeing a different person than the Susan Bowman I had been working with, a Susan who was very much a woman seeking approval, the tough shell of masculinity stripped from her.

"Thank you, Bob," she said softly.

I'd never had a woman thank me before and I didn't know what to say, so I just lay there, looking at her and wondering which person was the real Susan Bowman. For that moment I thought I was seeing the real one, a Susie who was soft and feminine and capable of a deep, feminine feeling, but it didn't last.

She stood up, brushing the sand from her body. "I had to find out how good you were," she said in a matter-of-fact voice.

This was the familiar Susie, hard and brash and working hard at being masculine. I got up and started dressing, a number of thoughts pounding through my head, words I wanted to say, but words I didn't dare say if I wanted to stay there.

She kept on rubbing her body, although all of the sand must have been gone before. The light was very thin, so I

83

couldn't see her face clearly. She said, "You like Janey, don't you?"

"Yes."

"Are you in love with her?"

"I think so," I said.

"She's never had a man," Susie said, still very matter-of-fact. "It's too bad, but she's never been like me. Too proper to enjoy herself. I've been so damned mad at this man's world we live in that I've had to prove I could do anything a man could. I guess I've proved what I can do, but Janey never seemed to have to prove anything. She submitted right from the first. Maybe she really liked doing the work a woman was supposed to."

She dressed slowly. I had pulled my boots on and then waited for her to dress. When she finished, she turned to face me. "I'll let Janey have you. Be good to her." I thought she said it enviously, and wondered if she honestly liked herself, or if she would rather have been like Janey.

We started toward the house. We were nearly there when Susie said, "I lied to you about wanting to find out how good you were. What I really had to do was to show you that I was a woman in spite of the way I act and talk. You weren't sure, were you?"

"No," I said.

"Well, you know now."

We went into the house through the living room. When we reached the kitchen, Janey was stirring the gravy. She said petulantly, "The supper's ruined."

"It's all right," Susie said. "We'll eat it the way it is."

I was startled. I had never heard Janey use that tone before. I sat down at the table, not looking at her. I knew she knew, and that she knew I knew, but neither of us ever mentioned it.

Chapter XV

As far as my mission to Smith's Cove was concerned, I was at a complete standstill. I didn't hear anything from Chip. Van Tatum apparently had left the country. Ned Rusk and Ash Morck had not come home.

But the work on the Rafter B went on. We irrigated. We finished cutting the wood. A man from the upper end of the Cove came with his circular saw that was hooked up to a gasoline engine, and sawed our wood into sixteen-inch lengths, then we moved it into the woodshed and stacked it against the back end between the walls. There were always chores to do, such as cleaning manure out of the stalls in the barn and from the corral. When I couldn't find anything else to do, I helped Janey in the garden, which was producing about everything we ate.

Now that my muscles had hardened up, I found our life a pleasant one and actually enjoyed the work, but Van Tatum's shadow always seemed to be upon us, with the foreboding suspense of not knowing when he'd come back to kill us. All three of us had the feeling that sooner or later he would try.

There was something else that bothered me, something I couldn't put my finger on, but I sensed it after that evening on the sand beach. Susie was not as arbitrary as she had been. Sometimes when we were working together she'd go for hours and not say a word. On occasion she would stop what she was doing and stare into space, standing motionless for as much as five minutes at a time.

I never said anything to Susie when she had one of those spells, but it bothered me because it wasn't like her and I wondered what was happening to her. Or she would watch me covertly when she thought I didn't know it. That didn't seem like her, either.

It came to a head late one afternoon when I was cleaning out the stable. We had knocked off a little early and had come in to move the wood rack off the wagon and replace it with the hayrack. We had sharpened the mower's sickle and oiled the machine so we could start haying in the morning.

I hadn't seen Susie for half an hour, but that didn't concern me because it was not unusual. She often had little jobs she attended to without saying anything to me, and she had stopped giving me directions because she knew I'd find something to do. Just as I was finishing the last stall, and had started to wheel a load out through the barn door, I heard something that I couldn't identify from the front of the barn on the other side of the granaries.

I put the wheelbarrow down and listened. At first I thought it was the big black cat that patrolled the barn looking for mice, but I didn't think it sounded like any cat I'd ever heard, a strange, moaning sound. I climbed out of the stall across the manger and walked around the side of a granary to the corridor that ran along the front of the granaries. The big door was open so there was plenty of light. Susie was sitting on a sack of oats, her face in her hands. She was crying.

It would be an understatement to say I was startled. I stood still for a full minute or more, then walked to her and sat down on an upended box in front of her. She wasn't aware of my presence for a time, but kept on crying, not the shoulder-shaking sobs that women have at times, but a low, keening sound of someone who is suffering a dull, inexpressible pain.

I suppose I sat there five minutes not knowing what to say or do. A crying woman had always made me uncomfortable, but I thought I ought to do something, so finally I said, "Tell me about it."

She looked up, startled, "Oh, my God," she said. "I didn't know you were here."

She wiped her eyes, and I repeated, "Tell me about it."

"I didn't want you to catch me," she said. "I didn't know you were anywhere around."

"Go on," I said. "Tell me about it. It will do you good to talk."

She dabbed at her eyes again, then she said in a tone so low I could hardly hear her. "I can't. Not because I don't want to. It's just that I don't know how to say it."

I could make a good guess what her trouble was. I'd had a hunch ever since that night beside the river, when I'd caught a glimpse of a woman who had tried to hide herself behind a masculine facade. I took a chance and said, "You're riding two horses, aren't you? You'd like just to be a woman."

Her eyes widened as she stared at me. "How did you know?"

"I've seen both sides of you," I told her. "You're a hell of a woman when you let yourself be one."

I put out a hand, thinking I could comfort her, but she leaned away, saying, "Don't touch me. I'd turn to jelly if you did."

She shook her head. "I can't face what you call being a woman. I wasn't raised to be one. Daddy wanted a boy, so he tried to make a boy out of me almost as soon as I was big enough to walk. I could do everything that Daddy could do, from branding a calf to cutting a pig. Damn it, Bob, I think like a man, and most of the time I act like a man. I'm not a man and nothing can change that, but how can I live like a woman?"

She paused, the tears close again as she relived her childhood. She went on, "Maybe I was naturally this way, or maybe it was because of the way Daddy raised me, but now I'm the way I am. I can't cook, I'm not worth a damn in the house, and I don't think I could even wash dishes if I tried.

"If you married Janey and took her away, I'd hire a man to do the work, but the hell of it is I couldn't keep house." She threw out her hands in an expression of despair. "What am I going to do, Bob? If you don't take Janey with you to Denver, we can't go on living this way. It's not fair to Janey. She wants to leave and I don't blame her."

"I'm not sure I'm marrying Janey," I said, "and taking her away. I'm not even sure she wants to go with me, or how she'd get along living in Denver, but you're right about one thing. You're not going to be able to live this way if Janey stays. You are a woman, Susie. I found that out." It was my turn to shake my head. "I don't know what you're going to do. It's too bad your dad raised you the way he did."

She gave me a half-smile, thinking again of that evening

beside the river. "I'm ashamed of what I did, Bob. I know a woman lets the man do the chasing, but I've done it so long that it's hard to keep from it."

"I understand that," I said. "Some men don't mind. Chip doesn't."

"You think I ought to marry him and start living like a woman," she said. "I can't, Bob. I just don't love him that way. I wish I did, but I'd never be contented to live a lifetime that way."

She rose, once again assuming the tough, masculine role she had lived for so long that it had become her normal state. She was ashamed she had let me see this chink in her armor. She never showed it again until the day she died.

Chapter XVI

We started haying the next morning. Susie ran the mower and the rake. As soon as the hay was cured, I shocked it. Later we hauled the hay to the barn and she worked the fork and I spread the hay in the mow. Janey led the horse that was hooked to the rope that pulled the forkfuls of hay from the load into the mow. It was the first time since I'd come to the Rafter B that she had done anything outside, and she wouldn't have done this if there had been any other way to handle the unloading.

"I don't mind," she told me one evening. "Daddy had me doing it when I was so small I could hardly reach the bridle."

The weather turned unbearably hot, over one hundred degrees by noon on every day we hauled. Janey got dusty and sweaty just as Susie and I did, but I guess she didn't mind because I never heard her complain. One afternoon when we were nearly finished she brought a pitcher of cool lemonade from the house before we started to unload. She poured a glass and handed it up to Susie who was on the load, then poured a glass for me. She filled her own glass last, but before she took a swallow, my glass was empty.

"Help yourself," she said, motioning to the pitcher she had set on the ground.

"I never tasted anything better in my life," I said. "You are an angel and I love you."

Startled, she pulled her glass away from her lips. "I wish I could believe that," she said.

I picked up the pitcher and emptied it into my glass, then set the pitcher on the ground next to the wall of the barn. I drained my glass and set it beside the pitcher, and when I looked at Janey, I saw tears in her eyes. On impulse I kissed her.

"Why not believe it?" I asked.

"I'm afraid to," she answered.

"Come on, you lovebirds," Susie said. "We're going to get a thunderstorm. Let's get this load into the mow."

I went inside and climbed the ladder to the mow. I knew I shouldn't have told Janey I loved her; I still wasn't sure I did, or that marrying her was the right thing to do. I'd thought about it a good deal the last few days, but I just couldn't make up my mind that it was right to break up the sisters by taking Janey to Denver, and I was less sure how Janey would feel, cramped up living in a house on a small lot in Denver, after spending her life on a ranch the size of the Rafter B.

The storm struck just after Susie and I put the team away, unharnessed, and reached the house. First there was lightning that seemed to split the earth, then the thunder that sounded as loud and terrifying as a cannonade prelude to a great battle, and after that the rain, a genuine gully-washer.

Susie and I stood at a window in the living room staring at the downpour while Janey finished supper. Susie said, "That was close. I'm glad we got in before it hit."

"We won't have to irrigate for a while," I said, "but it's hard on Janey's garden."

"She'll be sick," Susie said. "Don't mention it. Maybe she won't think about it."

She didn't. She had something else on her mind that kept her preoccupied through supper, but I didn't know what it was and she didn't say anything until we had finished her cherry pie, then she said, "I've got something to tell you that I'd rather not even think about. I'm scared."

"Say it anyway," Susie said impatiently. "You get scared too easy."

"Not about this," Janey snapped, showing an irritation with Susie I had never heard before. "Frisbee sent the Walton kid over with a message. Ned Rusk and Ash Morck are back."

Susie had lifted her coffee cup for a sip. Now her hand froze halfway to her mouth. "Well," she said angrily, "you're a long time telling us."

"Soon enough," I said. "We wouldn't be going out in this, and I'm glad we hadn't started before the storm hit."

Susie didn't argue. She shrugged and said, "We'll pull out as soon as we finish breakfast."

I didn't sleep much that night. If Van Tatum was still in the country, and I didn't have the slightest doubt that he was, we might be too late. If we weren't, I figured we'd run into him somewhere around the Morck or Rusk cabin. That prospect scared the hell out of me. We were amateurs. Susie would be as good a partner as a man, but two ordinary men bucking a professional like Van Tatum made poor odds.

I lay on top of the covers completely naked. The rain had stopped, but the air was hot and sultry, a sort of pressing heat that seldom came to a country as high as Smith's Cove. Sometime after midnight I heard my bedroom door open. I sat up, my heart pounding, until Janey said, "It's me, Bob."

It was the first time she had come to my room. I knew damn well why she was here, and I knew equally well I wasn't going to do it to her. Susie yes, but Janey, no. Not that I wouldn't have enjoyed it. I'd thought about it plenty of times and I always ended up knowing it would be a tragic mistake, Janey being the kind of woman she was.

She came to my bed. She was wearing a robe that she dropped when she reached the bed and lay down beside me, a hand touching me. She said, "I couldn't stand it, Bob, being alone and thinking about tomorrow. I'm afraid you won't come back."

"Quit worrying," I said. "I'll come back."

I wondered as soon as I said it whether I was lying to her or not. I did not feel as certain as I wanted her to think I felt. She pressed against me. It was too hot a night for this closeness, but I couldn't tell her that, so I put an arm around her and held her hard against me. One of her hands roamed over my body as she turned my face so my mouth was close to hers. She kissed me and I knew at once this was getting out of hand. Even on a hot night her soft, young body was too tantalizing to resist. I pushed her away, thinking that I had kissed a lot of women, but none of their kisses had ever aroused me the way hers did.

"I love you, Janey," I said. "I haven't told you because I've got a hunch that marriage isn't right for us, but damn it, you've got to quit this or we'll have to get married."

"I don't want to quit," she said. "What do you think I came up here for?"

91

"We're not going to do it," I said. "Don't make it hard for me."

"You don't know how it's been, having you here these weeks which seem like only a few minutes. It's . . . it's sort of like having a glimpse of heaven after living a boring and monotonous life that I had no hope of ever changing. I just can't bear the thought of you getting killed."

It was hard enough to say without having her put it that way, but I knew I had to say it. I simply had too many doubts about our future. "You don't have me now, Janey. If I married you and took you to Denver and you were unhappy living there, I . . . well, I don't know what I'd do."

"I'd be happy just living with you," she said. "I know I would."

"You don't know anything about a reporter's life," I said, "or his hours. A lot of times I wouldn't be with you for as much as twenty-four hours and you wouldn't know where I was or what I was doing."

"I'd try to understand, Bob," she said. "I'd try very hard because I know it's your way of life and I wouldn't have any right to change it."

No use to argue, I thought. We wouldn't know if marriage for us would work until we tried it. I guess that's the chance any couple takes, but I knew I couldn't risk it until I felt more sure of how Janey would respond to city living than I did now. Besides, there was Susie.

"What about Susie?" I asked. "We owe her something. She can't run this outfit by herself."

"I don't know what you think of Susie," Janey said bitterly, "but as far as I'm concerned, I don't owe her a damn thing. I was never given any choice about being her sister."

I was shocked. I had never heard her talk that way before, and suddenly it struck me that this bitterness I sensed went back to their childhood when Alec Bowman had rejected Janey and had made Susie his child, leaving Janey no choice but to become a lady. I realized now, and I was ashamed that I had been too insensitive to feel it before, that Janey's and Susie's partnership was one of necessity rather than one of sisterly love. I don't think Janey would have admitted it, and maybe she wasn't even fully aware of it, but I was sure that she actually hated Susie and the role that her raising and circumstances had forced upon her.

She started kissing me again, soft, nibbling kisses that

were demanding in a gentle, seductive way. Again I pushed her away, saying, "I might get killed tomorrow. I'm not going to leave you with my baby inside of you. You'd better go downstairs."

"No," she said. "I'm going to stay here in your arms. At least I would have that much."

She sighed and relaxed, my right arm around her, and a few minutes later I heard her soft breathing and knew she was asleep. We stayed that way until Susie's yell woke her: "Damn it, Janey, are you up there with Bob?"

Janey sat up. "Oh my," she whispered. "I didn't intend to stay so long." She raised her voice, "I'll be right down."

"I'll be damned," Susie said incredulously. "So you are up there."

Janey slipped into her robe and scurried across the room to the stairs. "It won't take me long to get breakfast," she said, and went down the stairs.

I lay there a while, hearing their angry voices. I could not make out what they were saying, but they were quarreling. I was shocked. I got up and lit the lamp, shocked because I had assumed they got along with each other better than this.

Chip had never mentioned it, but he must have known about this strange love-hate relationship between the two women. I dressed, blew out the lamp, and went down the stairs, knowing that I need not worry about separating them.

Chapter XVII

We ate breakfast by lamplight. Then, while Susie and I saddled up, Janey stuffed a sack with enough food to last us at least until we got back. I didn't think we'd be gone long, but I guess she did. Of course I didn't know the country, or what Susie intended to do.

Janey came out to the corral before we mounted and handed the sack to Susie, who tied it behind her saddle. She had given me a Winchester that I had slipped into the boot and she carried another one. When I looked at Janey, I saw she had been crying. I opened my arms to her and she literally threw herself into them, hugging me hard and kissing me.

"Let go of him," Susie said impatiently. "You're holding us up."

Janey let go, tears still running down her cheeks. She said defiantly, "I'd hold him forever if I could. If you had a lick of sense, Susie Bowman, you'd get more help, but no, you're going to do it yourself."

"You're damn right we're going to do it ourselves," Susie said roughly. "I suppose you'd have me go to the sheriff."

I mounted, lifted a hand in farewell to Janey, and rode away into the winey coolness of early morning, the smell of a wet earth rising to our nostrils. I looked back once, saw Janey standing beside the corral still staring at us and waved again, then went on. Susie was angry, but she didn't say a word until we were a mile or more from the house, then she asked in a tone she tried to keep normal, "Did you screw Janey last night?"

"No," I answered. "I wanted to, but I may get killed today. I didn't want to leave her with a fatherless baby."

"You're a fool, but you're an honorable man," she said sarcastically.

Oddly enough, I sensed that she was relieved. I asked, "Are you going to pick up anyone else?"

"No," she said. "We can do the job ourselves. Now that Chip isn't here, there's not a man in the Cove I would trust in a showdown."

She seemed to be trusting me, so I guess what she said was a compliment. We stopped at the store, and even at this early hour, old-man Frisbee was up. He came out when he saw us, saying, "I figured you two would be along."

"You know anything more?" Susie asked.

"Not a damn thing," he said. "Morck and Rusk came by yesterday and bought enough supplies for a month. Paid for it in gold." He spread his hands as if to say we could draw our own conclusions about where it came from. "Said they'd just got back. I told 'em about this Tatum feller, but they said they'd handle him if he bothered 'em."

"That sounds like them," Susie said. "If we're lucky, we'll be back before dark. If we are, we'll stop and let you know."

The old man nodded. "I ain't told nobody else. I figured you'd do just what you're doing." He looked at me suspiciously. "You figure this hairpin will be any help?"

He had a way of making my hair stand up the wrong way. "Old man," I said hotly, "why don't you saddle up and come along? Then you'll know she's got some good help."

Frisbee cackled. "He's got some spunk. No, I ain't saddling up. My riding days are over. You'll have to do this job without my help."

"Let's ride," Susie said impatiently, and turned her horse back into the road.

I caught up with her, saying, "If I was around here very long, I'd teach that old bastard a lesson in manners. You say he's your doctor and preacher?"

"He's all we've got." She glanced at me, amused. "He could learn some, all right, but he thinks he's looking after Janey and me, now that Pa's dead. He's not much of a preacher. Janey and I don't go to church very much, which makes him mad. He prays and reads the Bible and talks about how we'd better get right with God if we want to be saved."

"I suppose it gives the people a place to go," I said.

"That's right," she agreed. "Life gets pretty monotonous in the Cove. If it wasn't for a few school programs, and three or four dances a year, I guess we'd all get cabin fever. My trial was the biggest thing that has happened around here for years. Everybody went. They were camped all up and down the river, and both days they were standing in front of the courtroom waiting to get in. I suppose it will be the same with my next trial."

"Kind of like a community circus," I said.

"That's about it. You can't really blame them. We live in a little hole in the ground that's sealed off by itself. People here don't have much money, and not much hope for the future. Progress just seems to go on by." She smiled wryly. "Life in Smith's Cove is a dreary existence."

I wasn't so sure that progress was always good, but I didn't raise the point. It wasn't the issue now. I did ask, "Are they happy?"

"I think so. Most of them have kids. Raise crops. Throw a few head of steers into the pool herd in the fall, which gives them all the cash they ever have. It's a simple life and not many demands on us. Most of the men don't amount to a damn. They don't like to work. It's easier to go shoot one of Kirby's steers or a deer than it is to raise their own meat. It's a man's world in the Cove. Women are something to enjoy in bed. Like I said, lot of kids, but most of them die young. The men get the fun of starting them and women have the agony of bearing them."

I let the subject drop because of the bitterness in her voice. It struck me that what she had just said was the major reason why she lived the life she did. She'd decided that she might as well enjoy the activity in bed as well as the men.

As we rode upstream I had a chance to look at the ranches we passed. I began to understand the reason for Susie's bitterness. The women I saw were frowzy and unkempt, and were hanging out washing or working in the garden. The children were dirty, long-haired, and wearing clothes that were literally patches on patches.

Smith's Cove was a pocket of poverty largely because of the laziness of the men who lived here, or so Susie implied. She was a worker. Her dad must have been, too. I was curious about the difference between the Bowmans and the other inhabitants of the Cove, but I didn't pursue that, either.

"I had a hunch that old-man Frisbee knows Morck and

Rusk are rustlers, or bank robbers or outlaws of some sort," I said. "Does everybody here think the same?" When she nodded, I asked, "Why do you let them stay?"

"Why shouldn't we?" she asked scornfully. "They don't bother us."

Her answer told me a great deal about the Cove people, and why Judge Wirt was hell-bound to convict Susie. She was the glue that held them together. I had a notion that Wirt wasn't on Kirby's side, except that if Kirby wintered his herd in the Cove, the people living there would be driven out and a nest of lawlessness destroyed.

An hour or so after we left the store we began to climb, the cottonwoods giving way to a jungle of scrub oak with an occasional grove of aspens. The road had curled away from the river. I could hear it pounding away to my left so I guessed it was dropping fast in a series of falls or rapids.

As long as we had been in the Cove following the river, the road had showed considerable travel, but now it ceased to be a road. It was no more than a trail. Anything that Morck or Rusk had brought up to their cabins must have come by pack animals, because the trail was too narrow for a wagon.

"With a whole valley below them," I asked, "why did these men come up here to live?"

"I guess that's one reason why we figure they're outlaws. They say they like to live by themselves, but we always thought they wanted to be hard to find." She shrugged. "They're gone as much as they're here. They've got a right to live anywhere they want. Folks in the Cove like them. They never make any trouble for us, and they were backing me up when we turned the Kirby herd back."

"They succeeded in one thing," I said. "They are hard to find. Tatum would never have known where they live if Frisbee had kept his mouth shut."

We followed the twisting trail for another half-mile. It was noon and I was hungry. I started to say so when I discovered that the trail forked, one going on up the mountain, the second turning to our right. We pulled up and Susie pointed to the fork that led to the right.

"Morck lives down there," she said. "It's not more than a hundred yards, but you can't see it until you're right on it. We'll see him first, then..."

The crack of a rifle ahead of us and to our right shocked

both of us into momentary paralysis. Susie cried out, "Morck!" I came to in a hurry, forgetting all about my hunger pangs. I rolled out of my saddle in a hurry and scrambled off the trail into the brush.

"Get down," I hissed, "You're a clear target out there."

She obeyed, her face white. Hunkered down beside me, she said, "Looks like we're too late."

The bushwhacker was not far away. I whispered, "Maybe not. What's on up the mountain?"

"It goes on like this for half a mile," she answered, "then gets into some pines. The top isn't much more than a mile from here. Beyond that there's a series of timbered ridges. It's rough country. If Tatum gets into that, we'll never find him."

I motioned to the right. "What's it like down there?"

"A narrow canyon," she answered. "Morck's cabin is built against the far wall. He's got a spring right beside it that runs the year around. He's got a shed for his horse and a pole corral. That's all. Rusk's cabin is up the canyon a piece."

"Can you see Morck's cabin from any place in the canyon above him?"

She nodded. "You can see it from Rusk's cabin."

"Tatum must be up there near Rusk's place," I said. "That probably means he's killed Rusk. If that shot we just heard killed Morck, Tatum will take off. If he's not sure he finished Morck, he'll be moving downslope to find out. I'm going to nail him. He won't be expecting any interference."

She looked at me doubtfully. "What am I supposed to be doing all that time?"

"Stay here," I said. "If he's got Morck, he'll leave the country unless he decides to pay us a visit. He's not likely to leave any other way, is he?"

"No," she said. "It would be tough traveling. This is the only road."

"Then keep an eye out for him," I said.

Our horses were standing in the trail. I jerked the Winchester that Susie had given me from the boot, dropped into the brush, and began working my way upslope.

Chapter XVIII

It was no picnic worming my way through the oak brush. I couldn't risk taking a direct course; I tried to keep in the densest part of the brush because I had no idea where Tatum was. I could have covered the same distance in a fraction of the time if I'd taken the trail, but that would have been the height of idiocy. For all I knew I could run into Tatum any moment, and I'd be a dead man if I let him get the drop on me.

A moment later I heard a rifle crack again. Now I knew where he was. I was wasting time crawling through the brush. The trail was not far to the right. I plunged toward it through the brush, limbs raking my face, but I didn't slow up or stop.

I started running as soon as I reached the trail, my Winchester held on the ready. The trail swung sharply to the north, and a moment later I was on the lip of the narrow canyon, Rusk's cabin was directly below me. The motionless body lying in front of the door was probably him.

One horse was in the corral, another one was tied at the side of the cabin, and then I spotted Tatum lying belly-flat, his rifle in front of him, his gaze pinned on Morck's cabin down the canyon. I could have shot him without the slightest danger, but I hesitated. I had never shot a man, and to shoot one in the back was more than I could stomach, so I eased down the steep slope, hoping I wouldn't dislodge any rocks that would warn him. I told myself I wanted to take him alive.

I succeeded in reaching the bottom of the canyon before alerting him. I don't think I made a sound, but I suppose there is some sort of monitor in the brain of a man like Van Tatum that warns him of danger.

Moving with incredible spped, or so it seemed to me, Tatum sat up and whirled, his rifle in his hands. He brought it into line and fired, a snap shot that was wide of the mark, but it scared hell out of me. I was facing a killer who was shooting at me when only a minute before I could have killed him without running any risk. That is exactly what Tatum would have done if our roles had been reversed.

I fired from the hip, not the best way to use a rifle, but the only way I could. If I had taken time to bring it to my shoulder, I would have been on the ground with a slug in my brisket. My bullet, more from luck than any expertise on my part, hit him squarely in the chest and knocked him off his knees. His second shot, fired as he was falling, went ten feet over my head. He'd probably cocked the Winchester, and then pulled the trigger after he'd been hit.

Keeping him covered, I walked toward him. He was alive, but from the way the blood was pouring out of him, and the location of the bullet hole, he wasn't going to live long.

I knelt beside him, asking, "Did Judge Wirt hire you to kill Morck and Rusk?"

"Hell, no," he whispered. "He ordered me to scare 'em out of the country, but you don't scare men like that. He's a fool."

"Then Kirby hired you?"

"Sure."

"To kill me, too?"

"No. He...didn't...know...nothin'...about...you. That...was...my...idea."

"Kirby wanted Susan Bowman dead, didn't he?"

"Yeah. He...said...she...was...the...cause... his..."

He couldn't finish the sentence, but he'd said enough. His body jerked and his head turned an inch or two as all his controls left him. His Winchester which he had been clutching now fell from slack fingers. I rose and looked down at him.

A few seconds before he had been a tough and deadly man, and I wondered how many people he had murdered. I began to shake, suddenly realizing that I had killed him. I turned away and began to gag. I didn't have anything in my stomach to come up, but I couldn't stop retching for a minute or two.

I staggered to the cabin, then my knees gave way and I sat down in the doorway. I got myself under control and wiped my sweaty face with my bandanna, then I looked at Rusk's body that lay a few feet from me. I picked up an arm and felt for his pulse. Not a trace. His body was cold. He must have been dead for hours, then I wondered how Morck could have been alive a few minutes ago. He must have been gone and Tatum had waited here for him to show up.

I wondered about Rusk, too. He was wearing his drawers and a shirt that hadn't been buttoned. That was all. I guessed he had barely stepped through the door when Tatum had shot him. He must have been in a hurry to relieve himself and hadn't taken time to pull his pants on.

Hearing a noise on the trail above me, I looked up to see Susie running toward me, slipping and sliding and almost falling as she descended the steep trail. I rose and walked toward her, demanding, "What are you doing here? I told you to stay where I left you."

"I heard the shots," she said. "I had to know if you were alive."

I saw the worry in her face, so I said, "I'm lucky," and pointed to Tatum's body.

She faced me, an expression of resentment taking the place of the one of worry. "You pulled the wool over my eyes," she said accusingly. "You aimed to end it yourself all the time. You told me to stay there because you knew..."

"Now hold on just a damned minute," I yelled. "I admit I hoped I could finish it, but I figured there was a fifty-fifty chance that Tatum would get past me and you'd have to stop him. Morck may still be alive, but if Tatum had been sure he'd finished him, he'd have been coming down the trail hell for leather. I was in the brush. I couldn't have stopped him. As a matter of fact, I left you in a hell of a dangerous situation. I apologize for that."

She chewed on her lower lip, staring at me doubtfully, then she nodded as if accepting what I'd said. "All right. No use of us quarreling about it now. I'm just glad you're alive." She pointed at Rusk. "What do you make of him?"

I told her what I had guessed, adding, "Or maybe he heard something and stepped outside to see what it was. Now I think we'd better get down to Morck's place and have a look at him." I nodded at the narrow canyon below us. "Can we get there that way?"

"It's rough going," she said. "We'd better take the trail. It's longer, but it will take less time. Besides, we can pick up the horses."

We started up the trail, Susie turning her eyes away from the bodies. I suppose she had never been around anyone who had been shot. I had seen plenty of murdered men when on assignment in Denver, but I had never killed a man before, and even though Tatum was a bad man any way you looked at him, I didn't feel good about killing him. My stomach had settled down, but the prickles were still running up and down my back, the knowledge nudging me that I was alive only through the grace of God.

We found our horses and rode down into the canyon to Morck's cabin. We still couldn't see anything of him, so I dismounted and called, "Morck."

"Here."

The voice was so low I hardly heard it. I ran around the cabin. Morck was lying on his back, his eyes closed. I guess he thought I was the killer because he said in the same low, strained voice, "Get it over with."

Susie had dropped to her knees beside him. "It's Susie, Ash. We'll get you inside the cabin. We can fix up a travois and take you to Frisbee."

He opened his eyes and looked at her. He was a big, whiskery man. Maybe he was an outlaw, but I didn't get that feeling about him. He was in no way like Tatum, whose viciousness was a constant aura around him. Morck might have been any of the little ranchers in Smith's Cove. Perhaps that was the reason he had been accepted by the Cove people; he seemed like one of them.

Morck closed his eyes again. "No use, Susie. It's the end of the trail. Get me inside. I'd like to die in my own bed."

Susie took his feet and I picked him up by the shoulders and we carried him inside. He had been shot twice, once in the arm and once in the stomach. The latter was the one that was killing him. The bleeding couldn't possibly be stopped in time. He would have died even if we'd been in Canby and could have seen a doctor immediately.

He was groaning in pain; his face was gray with the pallor of death, but he lingered, his good hand pressed against his stomach wound as if somehow he could stop the bleeding.

"Rusk had been dead for hours," I said. "How long ago were you shot?"

He opened his eyes and looked at me. "Who is this hairpin, Susie?"

"Bob Norberg," she said. "He's a Denver reporter."

"He's got something to write about," he said. "I'd been out hunting, trying to get some camp meat, and had just got back. The killer was up there somewhere around Ned's cabin. His first shot broke my arm. I tried to make it inside, but he got me a second time. The best I could do was to crawl around the corner of the cabin."

I was surprised that he could talk that much, or even wanted to. It was obvious he only had minutes to live, but he was lucid. He was, I thought, a very tough man. I wished I had known him.

"The man who shot you is named Tatum," Susie said. "He's dead. Bob killed him."

"I heard the shots," he said. He closed his eyes again. "You're some reporter. Kirby behind this?"

"That's right," I said.

"I ain't surprised," he said. "He knew he couldn't convict us, so he had us murdered." He stopped, fighting for breath, then he said, "We've had some good times, Susie. You take the saddlebag. What's in it is yours."

He lifted his good arm and Susie took his hand. She held it, standing close to his bunk. A moment later he was gone. She was crying as she turned away.

"He was always as independent as hell," she said, "and so damned sure of himself. Always thought he could handle anything. Now he's dead."

"Was he your beau?" I asked.

She shook her head. "Not exactly, but I liked him. I liked him as well as any of them, but he wasn't a man to get married. He liked the kind of life he had."

I picked up the saddlebag from the floor and opened it. I said, "Look."

She swung around. "I don't care what's in it," she said. "I don't want it."

She looked, though, and I heard her take a quick, long

breath. It was filled with money, both gold and greenbacks. I couldn't tell how much was there, but I guessed more than $5,000.

"You'd better take it," I said. "Nobody knows where it came from, and there's no way of finding out with both of them dead. You can't give it back. You know what will happen if you give it to the sheriff."

"He has big pockets," she said. "I'll keep it for a while. Maybe we'll hear where it came from."

"I'll saddle his horse and we'll load him on it," I said. "What will we do with the bodies?"

"Frisbee will take care of them," she said. "We'll leave Tatum up here. Frisbee can send someone to bury him or he can rot."

I saddled Morck's horse and we carried his body outside and tied him face down across the saddle, then we mounted and Susie led his horse back up the main trail.

"Stay here," I said. "I'll get Rusk's body."

When I returned, I was carrying a second saddlebag. "You might as well have this one, too. Nobody is going to know anything about it. It won't be part of my story to the *Chronicle*."

She took it, not saying anything. I said, "I moved Tatum inside the cabin. I shut the door so animals can't get at him."

"Who cares?" she said bitterly. "He was worse than any animal that wants to eat. He murdered two good men today."

I didn't tell her he probably would have murdered her and me both if he'd lived long enough. I didn't argue with her statement about Tatum being worse than an animal. I felt the same way.

Chapter XIX

When we stopped at the store, old-man Frisbee came out, saw who the dead men were, and shook his head. "God forgive me," he said hoarsely. "I should have known that bastard wasn't their friend like he claimed he was. They've never had a friend stop to see them in all the years they've been living up there."

We stepped down, Susie asking, "You want the bodies?"

He sighed. "Bring 'em on back. I've got a couple of coffins that's big enough for 'em. I'll go take the lids off."

Susie and I pulled Morck off his horse and carried him through the store to the back room where Frisbee had the coffins. We laid him into one of them, then went back for Rusk.

"Tatum's dead," I said. "I put him in Rusk's cabin so the coyotes couldn't chew on him. You want to send somebody up there to bury him?"

"I sure don't want him stinking up our graveyard," he said. "We'll get him buried after we take care of our friends. We'll have to have the funeral tomorrow. They won't keep in this hot weather."

"What time?" Susie asked.

Frisbee thought on it a moment, then said, "Let's make it three o'clock. That'll give us time to get the graves dug." He scratched the back of his neck, studying Susie. "You plug Tatum?"

She jerked a hand in my direction. "Bob did it. Left me twiddling my thumbs in the trail while he went on up to Ned's cabin and shot it out with Tatum."

"I'll be damned." He looked at me with some respect for the first time. "That's more'n I gave you credit for."

"I know," I said sharply.

I thought of a few more choice words I wanted to say, but I didn't. I wheeled and walked out of the store. I'd had about all I wanted from that old goat. I mounted and started on toward the Rafter B, Susie catching up with me a minute later.

It was nearly dusk when we took care of our horses. We hadn't eaten since breakfast and suddenly I was ravenous. I'd lost my appetite when I'd had the set-to with Tatum, but I had it back now.

Janey ran out to meet us and hugged me, saying, "I'm so glad you're back. I've been scared ever since you left."

"You underestimate our friend Bob," Susie said. "He took care of Tatum. He's dead."

"Then he won't bother us any more," Janey said.

"Not unless his ghost does," I said. "I'm starved, Janey. Supper ready?"

"No, it's not," she flared, as if insulted. "How was I to know when you'd be back?"

"I guess you wouldn't," I said.

"I've got a good fire going," she said. "I'll get supper started right away. Did you eat your lunch?"

"No."

"Take a sandwich," she said. "It'll tide you over."

"I'll do that," I said.

I carried the sack of grub and Susie took the two saddlebags. We hadn't mentioned them to Frisbee and I wasn't sure whether he had noticed them or not. In any case, he hadn't asked. I dropped the grub sack on the kitchen table and fished out a roast-beef sandwich. Susie went into her bedroom with the saddlebags and left them there, not saying anything about their contents to Janey.

"I'm going for a swim," I said. "I guess I can get back in time."

Janey nodded. "It'll be an hour or so."

I had eaten the sandwich by the time I reached the river. I felt better as I took off my clothes and jumped into the water. The day had been hot and I was sweaty, but there was something else, a prickly, uneasy feeling, and a peculiar smell that was unfamiliar to me. I had smelled my own smells long enough to recognize them, but this one was new.

Maybe it was the stink of fear. I had never been as scared in my life as I was when I faced Van Tatum and his Winchester. Or maybe it was the smell of death. I hadn't known Rusk or Morck, but Susie had always spoken highly of them. Outlaws or not, they didn't deserve to die from Tatum's bullets. Or maybe the odor was my imagination, but I didn't smell it after I left the water and dressed.

I sat on the warm sand for a time staring at the black sheet of water in front of me. The darkness was complete now except for a few stars that had appeared, but they did little to illuminate a world that had no other light except the lamp in the window of the Rafter B ranch house.

A lot of thoughts pounded through my head during the few minutes that I sat there, thoughts about life and death, of Ike Kirby and how he could hire a man like Van Tatum to murder people and still escape the punishment that would have come to a poor man, and of the two women who were so much involved with my life. But mostly I thought about myself, or where I had been and where I was going, or how much a man's destiny is in his hands and how much is already written in the book.

Presently I heard Susie call, "Bob?"

I answered, "Here," and stood up.

"It's as black as the inside of a bull's gut," she said as she appeared before me. "I almost broke my neck a few times getting over here."

"You should have brought a lantern," I said, "or better yet, have let me find my own way back."

"There are a lot of things I should have done," she said gravely as she slipped an arm around me. "I just want to say I'm glad we're both alive. I thought I hated you for leaving me on the trail and going ahead and taking care of Tatum yourself, but I don't. It's kind of nice to be looked after. It's something I haven't experienced very often."

"I'll tell you one thing," I said. "You're one hell of a woman when you put your mind to it."

Neither of us said a word as we walked back through the darkness. Our arms were around each other, the first time since that evening beside the river that Susie had touched me in this manner. I had a very strong feeling that I was the first man who had shown Susie some of the courtesies that a woman ordinarily receives from a man, and that she liked it, that she was fighting a battle within herself as to whether she'd go on playing a man's role, or accepting that which nature had given her.

When we reached the house, she said softly, "I told you once that if you liked Janey, I'd leave you alone. I may change my mind."

She gave me a squeeze and withdrew her arm. When we crossed the living room to the kitchen, Janey looked at us suspiciously, but she didn't say anything. I guess she figured out that Susie hadn't been gone long enough for us to have done anything of an intimate nature.

Supper was a silent meal. Oddly enough, Janey did not ask anything about what had happened except to inquire when the funeral would be, and Susie told her tomorrow. I guess Susie and I were still a little scared and just plain thankful to be alive, but I don't know about Janey. She kept glancing at Susie, frowning as if something was bothering her, or as if she resented something that Susie had done, but she didn't say anything.

When we were finished, I rose, then stood behind my chair when Susie said, "I know we're both tired, Bob, and I suppose you want to go to bed, but I'd like for you to stay up a few minutes. I'll help Janey clear the table."

"Well," Janey said, "that's something different."

She was being sarcastic, but Susie didn't reply in kind. I sat back down and the two women had the table cleared in a couple of minutes, then Susie went into her bedroom and returned with the saddlebags. She emptied them on the table—the biggest pile of gold coins and greenbacks I had ever seen in my life. Janey sat paralyzed, her eyes wide and filled with disbelief.

When Susie dropped the saddlebags to the floor and sat down at the table, Janey blurted, "I didn't think there was that much money in one pile in the whole world."

"What are we going to do with it?" Susie asked.

"We'll spend it," Janey said instantly. "It can get us out of Smith's Cove. With that and what we can get for the Rafter B, we can travel. New York. Paris. London. We can go anywhere in the world."

"You don't even ask how we got it," Susie said. "And why do you think we'd ever sell the Rafter B?"

"Because we're not going to waste all of our lives in this godforsaken hole in the ground," Janey said passionately. "I'm not going to get old and gray working my ass off for nothing.

We've got a right to see some of the world, and not wear out the way our mother did."

"What makes you think you have a right to this money?" Susie asked. "Bob and I risked our lives to get it while you stayed home doing the housework?"

"Well, by God," Janey said in a low, tense voice, "is that the kind of thanks I get for doing the housework? You enjoy riding and cutting calves and making hay and playing at being a man, and you've always been happy for me to stay cooped up in here washing and ironing and cooking and scrubbing and breaking my back in the garden. I thought we had a partnership and would share and share alike." She rose and glared at Susie. "Now you've got the gall to ask me why I have a right to share the money."

She began to cry. She ran out of the kitchen and a moment later her bedroom door slammed shut. I looked at Susie who was staring at the top of the table, her face white, or as white as her dark tan permitted. I was shocked. I had never heard Janey curse before. I thought she had indeed been raised as a lady, and although I had the feeling she wasn't happy here on the Rafter B, I had never dreamed she had the crazy, pent-up hatred for Susie she had just showed, as the torrent of angry words had flowed out of her.

"I guess I didn't know Janey very well," I said.

"I was very much aware of that," Susie said, "but I knew it wasn't any use to tell you. You wouldn't have believed it if I had, but I guess I didn't know her as well as I thought I did. I didn't know she hated housework so much."

"Chip doesn't know her, either, does he?" I asked.

"Only partly," Susie said. "You see, for a long time Janey was happy and accepted her life of what Mama used to call 'being a lady', but after she died, Janey resented having to do the housework by herself.

"She hated Pa because he didn't want me to help her. He wanted me to be with him. After Pa died, she began hating me. The anger that you saw this evening developed in the last year. I guess she saw her youth leaving her and she didn't have any real hope of ever changing her life. Chip hasn't been home for a while, so he doesn't know how much she's changed."

Susie started piling up the coins and the greenbacks into hundred-dollar stacks. I helped her. After a time she said slowly and regretfully, "I don't really blame her, Bob. She's partly right. I had a chance to go East, which she never had. I make all the decisions about the ranch. I'm the one they arrested for stealing a heifer, not Janey. I've always had men chasing me. She sees herself as a slave girl."

When we finished counting, we found there was more than $11,000. Susie sat down and stared at it. "What will we do with it, Bob? Is it really ours to spend?"

"I don't want any part of it," I said. "My advice is to hang on to it for a while just to see if the law starts nosing around. I doubt that it will, since no lawman has seriously gone after Morck and Rusk. If you don't hear anything in, say, six months, go ahead and start spending it. There's no way under the sun that anyone can prove where the money came from. It's probably from some bank robbery, but what bank? It might even be from a job they pulled a year ago."

"I guess so," she said, as if still uncertain. "If folks knew about it, I suppose there'd be a hundred people claiming it who didn't have as much right to it as I have."

"That's right," I agreed, "so whatever you do, don't talk about it. Don't spend it at one time, either. That would make people suspicious about where it came from." I paused, then I asked, "What about Janey?"

"I don't know," she said. "I honestly don't know. There are plenty of improvements I'd like to make on the Rafter B. That is, if I used the money the way I want to and not the way Janey wants. We've barely made enough to live on since Pa died, and he didn't leave us any money. If I bought Janey out, I wouldn't have enough left to make any improvements."

I got up. "Let's do the dishes."

"Let's?" she said. "That's woman's work, Bob."

"Not if you've lived alone the way I've done," I said.

"I haven't touched a dish to wash it for months," she said.

"If you're going to run this outfit without Janey," I said, "you'd better start touching them."

"I guess so," she said, hesitated, then added, "I can swing it. If Janey and I can agree on a price. I don't think she's going to stay with me whether you marry her or not."

As I dried the dishes, I thought a little bitterly about how a man can fall so easily into the trap of idealizing a woman and being fooled by her. Susie was right. If she had told me about

Janey's temper, I wouldn't have believed her. I was glad it had happened. I couldn't marry any woman with a temper like Janey's.

Chapter XX

I slept late the following morning. I had never been so completely worn out in my life. Usually Susie yelled at me to roll out before sunup, but she didn't this morning. It was full daylight when I woke, and at first I thought something was wrong. I dressed and went downstairs to find Janey alone in the kitchen. She had set the table, but two plates were dirty.

Usually Janey was very pleasant in the morning, and would always give me a smile and sometimes a kiss, but this morning she didn't say good morning. She looked at me as if I were an intruder.

"Sit down," Janey said in a cranky voice. "I'll fry your eggs."

She was sullen. Her eyes were red, and I wondered if she had been crying all night. I sat down and she poured the coffee. I didn't say anything and she didn't, either. A few minutes later she brought a slice of fried ham and two fried eggs to the table, then a plate of biscuits, and left the room. I ate by myself, wondering what in hell had happened to her. Sure, she'd been as sore as a stepped-on bull calf last night, but I didn't think she'd keep her bad temper this long.

I left the house when I finished eating and went out to the barn where I found Susie sitting on a milk stool. She looked at me and grinned a little, and said, "I thought you were going to sleep all day."

"I fooled you," I said. "What's going on?"

She didn't answer for a time, but picked up a length of straw, folded it over and over until it was an inch long, then she threw it away, picked up another piece, and did it all over again.

"Janey's having one of her mad spells," Susie said finally. "She woke me up before daylight and wanted to know if I'd changed my mind. I got contrary, being sore at her for waking me up at that time of night. I said no. We argued a while, then I got up and dressed and went out to milk. Janey had breakfast ready when I got back to the house.

"We ate, then we argued some more, both of us getting madder and madder until we both lost our temper. Finally she threw a plate at me and I hit her a good wallop on the side of the head and came out here."

I couldn't believe it. Sure, I had seen another side of Janey last night, but I didn't fully believe it was the real Janey I was seeing, but now I wasn't sure which was the real Janey.

"Do you have these fights very often?" I asked.

"We didn't used to have them at all," she said. "Not as long as Pa was alive, but we've had several since. I don't think Chip ever saw us have one because Janey always let him see her good side. After he left we had some. I always wind up hitting her and I'm ashamed because I'm so damned big, but, my God, she can be vicious with her tongue when she tries."

"You can't live this way," I said.

"I know it," she said. "I think the whole thing is, she's decided this is no place to spend the rest of her life. I'd be happy to live my life out and die right here, but not Janey. She's read a lot of books and magazines about cities and other countries and she says she's going to see them before she dies."

"Let her go," I said. "You can hire a woman to keep house if you want to go on living the way you have been."

"I've about decided that," she agreed. "After the funeral I'll tell her that we'll go to town and get Judge Wirt to draw up the papers that we need. She can give me her share of the ranch, and I'll go to the bank and see how much I can borrow. If she'll take it for her part of the ranch, we'll make a deal. I don't know what I'll do if she won't go along."

"I can't believe this is the same Janey I thought I was in love with," I said. "She was too good to be true."

"That's right," Susie said. "What you didn't know was that to her you are the ticket for getting off the Rafter B and going to Denver. Sometimes I think she's possessed by a demon. She really is two women, Bob. When she's good the way she has

113

been since you came, I couldn't ask for a better sister. When she's the way she is now, I'm afraid of her.".

I had read about people being possessed by demons. I had also read about people having two personalities, but I had never run into that, either. Now I was beginning to believe I had met up with both.

"I'm going to split some wood," I said.

"Stay out of the house," Susie advised. "When she gets on a tear like this, I stay clear of her until she gets over it."

I spent the morning cutting wood. I didn't see Susie until she stopped by the woodshed on her way in from the barn. Janey had dinner ready. She said curtly, "Sit down as soon as you wash up."

We did. We ate in silence. When we were finished, Susie rose and nodded at me. "Bob, you hook up the hack and bring it around to the front of the house about half past two."

I said all right. Susie left the room. I shaved standing in front of a small mirror hanging on the wall near a window. When I finished, Janey said defiantly, "I suppose you think I'm terrible. Well, you've never been a fifth wheel all your life with all of your Pa's favors going to your sister, have you?"

"No," I agreed. "I haven't."

"It's been hell," she said. "I'm going to leave. I told you once that there was a big world out there I've never seen. I'm going to see it."

I walked to her and took her hands. "Janey," I said, "I've seen that big world. It's not that great."

"But I've got to see it," she said. "Don't you understand, Bob?"

"Yes," I said. "I think I do."

I went upstairs and put on a clean shirt, all the time thinking I had never met anyone I felt as sorry for as I did Janey Bowman. I was sick when I thought about what that big world did to people like her. I had seen too many of them in the red-light district.

I had the hack in front of the house at half past two. I was surprised to see Susie wearing a dress. It was the first time I had seen her in one. It wasn't a fancy dress, or even a Sunday dress, just a gingham one with a pink design that ran up and down and made her look taller than she was. I had the impression it was new, or at least that Susie had never worn it more than two or three times.

Susie was obviously embarrassed when she saw me staring at her. She said, "All right, I do own a dress."

"You look good," I said.

"Real feminine, I suppose." She stepped into the front seat. "Janey's coming."

I had been wondering if she would. A moment later she came out of the house and stepped into the back seat as if she knew that was where she belonged. She had put on a dark green dress that rustled as she walked. It was far from new, and I had wondered if it had belonged to her mother.

She didn't say anything, just sat with her hands folded, her gaze straight ahead, the sullen expression still on her face. Perhaps it was a proper expression for a funeral. Folks might think it was one of sorrow.

I drove, and that was a little surprising. On any other occasion Susie would have reached over and taken the lines from my hands. Things were happening now, things I didn't fully understand, but I had a hunch that life was changing permanently on the Rafter B.

A large crowd was already at the schoolhouse. I tied at the hitch rail and we went in, but there were no seats, so we had to stand just inside the doorway. It was the first chance I'd had to see the Cove people, except for the glimpses I'd had on our way to Rusk's and Morck's cabins.

My feeling that Smith's Cove was a pocket of poverty didn't change, but my opinion of the people did. They were clean. The children's faces had been scrubbed until they were rosy-cheeked, the men were shaved, and obviously their wives had done some hacking on their hair.

Frisbee sat in the front of the room behind the coffins. Precisely at three o'clock he rose, prayed for the souls of the dead men, asking God to admit them into His royal domain, then he sat down and a fat, gray-haired woman moved from a front seat to the piano and played and sang two hymns. When she finished, Frisbee got up and talked for maybe ten minutes, saying that no one knew the history of the two men who were being buried, but no one cared. They had been good neighbors and the people in the Cove would miss them. He recited a number of neighborly acts they had done, ending with the help they had given turning back Kirby's herd.

When Frisbee finished, people began filing past the coffins, and then moved on outside the building to stand in the hot, afternoon sunlight. Susie and I had no reason to view the bodies, so we stepped outside and waited for Janey, who joined the procession moving past the coffins. A few minutes later the pallbearers carried the coffins outside and set them down beside the open graves.

The graveside ceremony was very brief, with Frisbee saying that we who were left to mourn the departed would miss them, then he committed their souls to God's loving care. He stepped back, the coffins were lowered into the graves, and then several men picked up shovels and began filling the graves.

The sound of clods and rocks hitting a coffin had always made me feel uneasy. I'm not sure why, except that it impressed me as sticking the dead into the ground to get rid of them so they'd be out of sight. I guess cremation and scattering the ashes over the earth to be warmed by the sun and swept away by the wind was a better response to death than the ordinary funeral and burial.

I walked away and stood by the hack. I was ready to leave, but I had to stand there through what seemed a long wait while the men shook hands with Susie and Janey and the women kissed them. As I watched, I had the feeling that the death of Ash Morck and maybe Ned Rusk, too, had meant more to Susie than she admitted.

Not many people paid any attention to me. A few shook hands and said they were glad I had killed the assassin—that Susie and I should have asked for help, but it turned out all right anyway.

The crowd began breaking up. Janey came to the hack and stepped up into the back seat again. She said, "This is where I always rode with Pa and Susie when we went anywhere. Can you understand what that meant to me?"

She had lost the sullen expression. She looked at me, a hint of a smile on her lips. I nodded and said, "Yes, Janey, I think I do."

"It's why I've got to see the big world we've been talking about," she went on. "I've got to see if there is a place for me that isn't in the back seat."

"I hope you find it," I said.

"I'll find it," she said, her lips firmly pressed together, her expression one of grim determination. "You'll see."

Susie had gone into the store for the mail. She came out

with a letter to me from Chip, asking me to come to Canby as soon as I could. He was going to Hicks and wanted me to go with him.

Chapter XXI

The ride to Canby was a long one. I got lost a couple of times when the road forked. Once I was out of the Cove, the sagebrush flat seemed to run on and on to distant mountains. When I say "road," I compliment the wheel ruts that took off in a general southeast direction.

When I had been with Chip, I had simply ridden along with him without paying much attention to anything we passed or to any of the forks. Once, when I went the wrong way, I came to a good-sized spread. I started to turn back, then I saw a sign ahead and rode on another fifty yards to see what it said. I made out the one word, "Hatchet," and remembered Chip telling me it was Kirby's outfit.

I reined up and studied the buildings for a time. I didn't see anyone, then I remembered somebody, I think it was Chip, saying that Kirby wasn't here much of the time. I did see two horses in the corral, and smoke was coming out of the ranch-house chimney, so the place wasn't deserted. Having no desire to see Kirby now, I turned and rode back, and this time managed to take the right turn.

Reaching town, I reined in at the livery stable where Chip worked. I didn't see anyone. I dismounted and yelled, "Chip?" I still didn't see him, so I led Prince along the runway to the back door. Chip was working with a sorrel gelding in one of the corrals. I yelled again. He turned and saw me, and yelled back, "I'll be there in a minute. Put Prince in that back stall."

By the time I had off-saddled, Chip was standing in the runway. He shook hands with me when I joined him, saying, "I wasn't sure you'd come. I figured you were having so much fun with the two women that you'd stay right there, and Denver would never see you again."

"It hasn't been that much fun," I said. "Susie and Janey send their love and don't think you should take the job at Hicks. You'll be so far away you'll never get out to the Rafter B again."

His face turned grave. "Maybe I won't, at that. I had intended to go sooner than this, but like a damn fool I kept hoping Susie would write and say to come back and we'd get married. I had a hell of a good time when I was out there, then all of a sudden Susie was tired of me. I just can't go back there, Bob. I'd get to hoping again and find that hope is all it is."

"You going in the morning?" I asked.

He nodded. 'I've told the boss, so after today I'm out of a job. I figured I'd go whether you showed up or not."

"What time do you plan to leave?"

"Oh, we ought to be moving out about seven," he answered.

"I'll be here," I said. "I've got a lot to tell you, but it'll wait. Right now I've got to see Judge Wirt."

"You'll have to get a move on," he said. "He's usually out of his office before now."

"I'll go to his house if I don't catch him at his office," I said. "I've got to see him."

I checked in at the hotel, washed up in my room, and ran most of the way to Wirt's office. I caught him just as he was getting ready to leave, and it was obvious he wasn't very happy to see me. He held out his hand, saying, "It's almost time for my supper, Norberg. I hope this visit won't take long. If you're here to plead Susie Bowman's case, we might just as well terminate our conversation right now."

"I'm not here for that," I said sharply. "I've got several things to tell you. Your supper's going to have to wait."

He sighed and motioned to a chair. "Sit down. I don't know what's important enough to make me miss my supper, or let it get cold..."

"Van Tatum is dead," I said. "That'll do for openers."

He had reached his swivel chair when I said that. He sat down quickly as if his knees had just given way under him. For a time he didn't say anything, but sat there staring at me. Finally he said, "You sure?"

"I'm sure," I answered. "I shot him."

"I guess you have got something to tell me," he said. "How did it happen?"

"First, I have a question to ask," I said. "How much did you have to do with bringing Tatum to Tremont County?"

The question shocked him. He had been looking at me, but now he turned his head to stare across the room. He said, in a voice that didn't carry any conviction: "Nothing."

"You had a meeting with Tatum in Denver just before he showed up here," I said, "along with Kirby and a third man. What was that meeting about?"

He reminded me of a kid who had just been caught with his hand in the cookie jar. He sputtered, reached for a cigar, then dropped his hand. He rose and walked to a window. He asked over his shoulder, "How did you hear that?"

"My boss has spies all over Denver," I said. "He doesn't miss much. He told me about the meeting just before I left."

"I could deny it, but I've always found that lies get me into more trouble than the truth. I was at that meeting, but my orders to Tatum were designed to scare some of the more notorious rustlers out of the county. They've been harbored too long in Smith's Cove. I have realized for some time that the sheriff will never bring them in, or if he did, he wouldn't have enough evidence to convict them. I thought a man like Tatum might make it so hot for them that they'd leave."

"You're naive," I said. "Men like that don't scare. Now they're both dead. Tatum murdered them just before I shot him."

I told him what had happened, starting with Tatum spying on us and then shooting at us as he left. He held up a hand, and when I stopped, he said, "Norberg, believe me, I had nothing to do with that. When I saw Tatum, I had never heard of you, and I certainly didn't and don't want Susan Bowman murdered. I want her kept alive to stand trial. We can convict her on the evidence we have. I'm hopeful it will serve as a warning to other people in the Cove." He motioned with one hand. "Go ahead."

I finished, leaving out two things: the saddlebags and their contents, and the fact that Tatum had exonerated Wirt from any blame for the murders he had committed. I thought it wouldn't hurt the Judge to stew a little on the latter.

He actually began to tremble. I had a good deal of respect for Oscar Wirt the first time I had met him, and I had been impressed by the way several Canby people had talked about him, but now I was aware that he was little different from me or the voters who had put him in office. He was just plain scared that he was going to be implicated in the death of the two men he had wanted to scare out of Tremont County.

He put a cigar into his mouth and chewed on it, his fingertips doing a steady tattoo on the top of his desk. After what seemed to me a long silence, he said, "Norberg, are you going to crucify me in your newspaper?"

"No," I said.

"You could, you know," he said bleakly. "My reputation would be ruined all over the state. I should have known not to get involved with that Goddamned Ike Kirby."

"Why did you?" I asked.

"Right now I wonder about it myself," he said. "I regret it like hell, and anything I say wouldn't really answer your question. It's just that I have worked so hard to establish law and order in Tremont County, but I've been stuck with a do-nothing, inept sheriff. When Susan Bowman was brought in, I saw a chance to start the ball rolling. People would know that at least one petty rustler would go to prison, and I hoped the rest would get the message.

"Regarding Kirby, it was just that with both of us being cattlemen, we had common interests. I was talking to him one day, and I said I knew there was no possible way we could convict Morck and Rusk even though they're admitted law-breakers. Then he said he knew how to get rid of them, and asked me to come to Denver where he and his foreman would be on that particular date. I had some business to do in Denver anyhow, so I went to the hotel room he mentioned. Kirby and his foreman were there with Tatum.

"At the time I didn't know who Tatum was or anything about his reputation, but he told me he'd done jobs like this and showed me some letters of recommendation he had from some cowman in Montana. He wanted half of his money down and the other half when I was satisfied that the men were gone. He said he'd leave for the Cove in the morning. We shook hands and I left the hotel. So help me God, Norberg, I had no idea he would murder those two men. All he said was, 'I know how to scare the living hell out of your rustlers. They'll soon be gone.'"

"They're gone, all right," I said. "One thing, Judge. How did you know Morck and Rusk were rustlers?"

"They admitted it," he said. "I have spies in the Cove, just like your boss has spies in Denver. Both men had talked about their exploits. Of course the Cove people looked on them as Robin Hoods about the same as they used to look at Cassidy and the Wild Bunch. The one job they did that has Kirby boiling is running off about a dozen of his best horses, including a stud that was worth a fortune. I was the one who told him who did it. Of course the Cove people applaud anything that hits Ike Kirby."

"How do you account for what Tatum did if it wasn't part of your agreement with him?"

"That's easy," he said bitterly, "now that I know what happened. Kirby gave the order after I left the room. He figured I couldn't complain once it was done. I'd be tarred by the same brush he was if I made it public. He's right, too."

I rose, but I stood there for a moment studying Wirt's bronze, handsome face that showed worry, a worry that hadn't eased up during our conversation. I thought he was telling the truth, but I decided not to tell him that Tatum had exonerated him. It might be good for Susie if he never knew.

"Judge," I said, "I can't understand why you didn't sense the kind of man Tatum was. I've seen some pretty bad men in Denver doing police assignments, but I never saw one that looked as vicious as Tatum. If I could believe in a literal devil, I'd say he'd look just like Tatum."

"You're exaggerating," Wirt said, "but I did feel uncomfortable sitting there talking to the man. Yes, I should have guessed—or at least looked up his record."

I walked to the door, then stopped. "Do you know where Kirby is now?"

"He's around here somewhere," Wirt said, "either in his house in town or out at Hatchet. He was in Canby at noon. He's bringing in a new band of horses and he wants to be on hand to look them over when they get here, so he's probably out at Hatchet."

I'd had the idea in the back of my mind that I'd ride by Hatchet on my way back from Hicks, but I could decide that later. I said, "I'll let you go get that supper you were worried about."

I opened the door, then closed it when he rose and walked slowly toward me. He said, "Norberg, do you have any notion of blackmailing me into dismissing the charge against Susan Bowman?"

"No, I hadn't thought of it," I said.

"Don't try it," he warned. "It won't work. If it comes to resigning and having my reputation ruined, I'll let that happen rather than allow the Bowman woman to go free."

I could respect him for that, at least. I thought he might really have been naive in accepting Tatum's word that he would do no more than scare Morck and Rusk. He had lived here in this isolated corner of Colorado, where he had not been exposed to the kind of vicious law-breakers I had seen so often in Denver.

"It won't be any problem for you," I said, and this time when I opened the door I stepped through it and left Wirt's office, leaving him standing there staring at me.

Chapter XXII

As late as it was, I didn't expect to find Sheriff Ed Allen in his office, and I didn't expect to get any satisfaction out of him if I did find him, but I had to try. I was wrong on the first count and right on the second. I walked to the courthouse right after I left Judge Wirt and strode along the hall to the sheriff's office in the back. Allen had just come out of one of the cells and was hanging up the keys when he turned and saw me. He was, to make an understatement, not delighted by my appearance.

"In case you don't remember me..." I began.

"Oh, I remember you, all right," he said. "You were in your drawers, but I remember you." He dropped into the swivel chair behind his desk, a scowl wrinkling his fat face. "I thought I told you to get out of town, that we don't want any nosy Denver reporters digging into our affairs."

"Oh, you told me, all right," I said, wondering if he was smart enough to know I was mimicking him. "I did get out of town, but now I'm back because I've got a report to make and a request. I've been staying on the Rafter B. Van Tatum, the man who tried to kill me and the man you didn't even try to find..."

"Now you just hold on a Goddamned minute," he interrupted angrily, "and you can stop insulting me. I didn't know who tried to kill you, if anybody did, and I'd like to know how you're so sure it was this Tatum hombre."

"He was staying in the mountains above Smith's Cove," I said, knowing there wasn't any use to explain how I knew what I knew. "On his way in he stopped at the Bowman place and took some shots at us. He had been ordered by Ike Kirby to murder

124

Susan Bowman, but we, me and Chip Morgan, spotted him and ran him off. He rode on upriver and hid out in the timber until Morck and Rusk got back home, then he shot and killed both of them. I killed Tatum when he tried to kill me."

Allen's mouth dropped open, and he was staring at me in the disbelieving manner of a man who has just heard a fairy tale. He said coldly, "I don't believe a word of what you're saying, and the charge that Ike Kirby ordered Susan Bowman or anyone else murdered is outrageous and libelous."

"I don't care what you belive," I said. "You can ride out to Smith's Cove and talk to Susie or Janey Bowman, and you can stop at the store and talk to old-man Frisbee, and then you can go to the cemetery and dig up a couple of new graves. We buried Morck and Rusk yesterday."

He leaned back in his chair and regarded me with cold, unfriendly eyes, as if the truth wasn't in me. "Maybe I'll do that," he said, "though I wouldn't believe the Bowman women any more than I believe you. I'm sure Susie's a liar and I know you are."

I was getting sore again, just as I had been the morning he barged into my bedroom. There was something about this fat, obnoxious man that aroused every hostile cell in my body. I had a notion he was the kind who tried to bully everyone except Ike Kirby and maybe Judge Wirt.

"You are an insulting son of a bitch," I said hotly. "If I lived in this town, we'd have an understanding."

"We're going to have one right now," he snapped. "I told you once to get out of town and I'm telling you again. If you're still here by noon tomorrow, I'll throw you in the jug for . . . loitering."

I laughed. I couldn't help it. Of all the absurd charges, that was the poorest he could have thought up. I hadn't been still long enough at any time since I'd been in Canby to be accused of loitering, but Ed Allen was not overly bright and I guess it was the only thing he could think of at the moment.

"You'd have a little trouble making that stick," I said. "Now about the request. Tatum lived for a few seconds after I shot him. He told me that Ike Kirby hired him to go to the Cove and murder Morck and Rusk. Also Susan Bowman. He intended to get her on his way out of the Cove. Me, too, I suppose. My request is that you arrest Ike Kirby for conspiring to murder."

Allen's face turned red. He sputtered a moment before he could get any words out, then he shouted in a tone of total outrage, "I have heard some wild and crazy ideas in my life, but this tops 'em all. I figured you were loco the first time I saw you. Now I know you are. You have no proof whatever as to what this fellow Tatum said, if he said anything. Your word wouldn't go very far in a Tremont County court. Now get to hell out of here. Maybe I can't hold you for loitering, but I sure as hell can hold you for insanity."

"I expected this from you," I said. "I know you weren't even worthy of the title of sheriff when I saw you in my hotel room. But there is one thing you can do, if you've got the guts to do it. Ask Kirby why he was in Denver several weeks ago having a talk with Tatum."

I wheeled and strode out, my blood pounding in my head. I have never considered myself a violent man, but I was close to violence right then. I don't think I'd have used my gun on Allen, but if I'd stayed and we'd exchanged one more insult, I would have used my fists, and I'd have pounded his jelly-like belly into a bigger mess of jelly than it was. If I had, he'd have had the excuse he needed to throw me into jail.

As sheer luck would have it, I ran into Ike Kirby just as I stepped through the front door of the courthouse. My temper, already shoving me near the edge of my self-control, went berserk when I saw Kirby. I grabbed the man by his shoulders and shook him.

"Morck and Rusk are dead," I yelled at him. "I guess that's what you wanted. They were murdered by your man Tatum. Now, are you going to send for another paid killer? You'll need one if you're going to finish off Susan Bowman, because Tatum is dead."

Kirby was too astonished for a moment to resist. When he recovered his wits, he cursed me and yanked free. He was carrying a gun and he could see I was wearing mine. I was no part of a gunslinger, and I don't have the slightest doubt that he could have smoked me down if he had gone for his gun and the law would never have touched him.

In spite of his red hair and hard blue eyes and imperious manner, he didn't have the guts. I'm not sure why, because I knew he was a tough man who had built his cattle empire largely by his own efforts, so he couldn't have lacked the courage. But maybe he was too shocked by my temerity to react in his normal way. I'm sure he hadn't been talked to for many years as I had just talked to him.

He backed off and glared at me, his face contorted by fury. When he didn't draw, I said, "Go ahead, make your play." For that wild moment, maybe I was impelled by a death wish. I don't know, but I do know I was goaded by a crazy recklessness I hadn't felt since I was a child.

I still couldn't leave well enough alone. I went on, "You said the last time I saw you that I had just committed suicide. Now see if you can make it stick."

He didn't try. I guess there were several possible reasons why he didn't. I'll never know what they were. He simply turned and strode along the hall into the sheriff's office, the back of his neck fiery red.

I must have raised my voice more than I thought, because people in the nearby offices had heard me. The late afternoon was hot and the doors along the hall were open. As I stared at Kirby's back, I realized that a dozen or more people had come into the hall to see what the shouting was all about. They had heard and seen what had passed between us, so the incident would be common knowledge by morning, a situation that a man like Kirby could not abide until I was dead.

As I left the courthouse, I realized I had been an idiot. I hadn't done myself any good. I'd rubbed Kirby's nose in the dirt and for the moment I had got away with it, but all I had really done was to add to Kirby's hatred of me, and make more certain than ever that he'd square accounts one way or another—probably with a hired assassin's bullet.

I walked to the hotel, thinking about it, and decided that if I was a gambling man, I wouldn't bet two cents on my survival. He might try to kill me tonight, or have someone else try the way Tatum had tried once before. He wouldn't know I was headed for Hicks tomorrow, so if I survived the night I'd stay alive for another twenty-four hours at least, but sooner or later I had to go back to the Cove, and that was probably where I'd get it.

I had been critical of Morck and Rusk for not being more alert to Tatum's presence, but the truth is that there was simply no defense against a dry-gulcher who shoots a man from ambush. That was the situation I was in. I'll have to admit that for a few minutes I was tempted to catch the night train for Denver.

The temptation didn't last long. I was too deeply

THE CATTLE QUEEN FEUD

committed. I had to stay for a few more days at least. If I was going to be murdered, then so be it. I was boxed in, and for a few crazy seconds I had a haunting feeling that my fate was predestined and I was helpless to control my future. It was not a philosophy I had ever subscribed to, so I tried to put it out of my mind.

I spent the next two hours in my hotel room writing my dispatch to the *Chronicle*, then added a note to Sid Gorman that I would be back in Denver in a few days, that I had seen and done and heard all I could until the trial. I would come back later in the summer for that.

By the time I finished, it was full dark, and when I considered Kirby's feelings for me, I decided it would be stupid to go out now. That would give Kirby the opportunity he was looking for. I went downstairs to the dining room and ate a late supper, taking care to sit at a table in the back of the room, as far from the windows as possible.

I was finishing my dried-apple pie when I saw Judge Wirt come in, glance around the dining room until he saw me, then come to my table. I motioned for him to sit down, curious about this visit. He had an expression on his face I couldn't identify. He was worried, or scared, or maybe both.

"I'll buy your supper," I said, "to pay you back for making you miss yours."

He shook his head. "Thanks, but I had supper a little while ago." He made an effort to smile. "My wife held supper for me until I got home, so it was late, but it wasn't cold." He leaned forward and lowered his voice, "Norberg, I don't know whether you are a hell of a brave man, or a plain idiot, but what did you accomplish by making Kirby look like a damn fool this evening?"

"Nothing," I said, "and I'm sorry I did it. I'm not usually cursed with a bad temper. But Ed Allen had just made me so damned mad by the way he dismissed everything I told him, and calling me a liar to boot, that when I saw Kirby, all I could think of was that the bastard had hired Van Tatum to commit murder and that I or one of the Bowman women could have been among his victims. . . . Well, I just plain blew up. I wanted him to pull his gun on me so I could try to kill him. I guess I went a little crazy."

He nodded, as if understanding, then he said, his voice still low, "I have faced the same situation with Kirby for years.

We're on the same side, but we have an opposite set of moral standards. I know what Kirby has done, but even in my position I can't stop him. I've tried to stay alive and figure out a way to handle him. I never have, and now you come along and set yourself up as a target. There is no way Kirby will forgive or forget you."

"That's the way I figured it," I said. "I just wish I could have it out with him personally, but he had his chance this afternoon and he didn't take it."

"He's got so used to hiring his killings done that he doesn't think of stomping his own snakes," Wirt said. "But he'll get them stomped. That's one thing you can count on." He glanced around to see if anyone was close enough to hear, then he went on, "That's why I'm here. I wish you'd get out of town tonight. If he has you killed in Denver, that's somebody else's bailiwick, but if it's done in Tremont County, we'll have reporters from every newspaper there is in Denver storming in here. I don't want that."

He glanced around again, then he whispered, "Kirby went into Allen's office and told him to kill you, that you weren't to leave town alive, then he walked out. Allen said he had never seen Kirby so furious. Now Allen doesn't know what to do. He says he just can't murder a man because Kirby told him to, but he's afraid not to do what Kirby ordered him to."

I almost laughed in his face. I thought it was the height of something for Kirby to order his hand-picked sheriff to do his killing for him.

"Sorry, Judge," I said. "I'll leave town in the morning. I can't do it tonight."

The Judge was a hell of a lot more worried about his community and its reputation than he was of my health. On the other hand, I was more worried about the latter. That night I slept with my bed shoved against the door.

Chapter XXIII

We had barely left Canby the following morning when Chip blurted, "What in the hell got into you to twist Ike Kirby's nose the way you done yesterday?"

"How did you hear about it?" I asked.

"It's all over town," he said. "You don't expect to do a trick like that and have it go unnoticed, do you? A dozen people in the courthouse heard you. You did it once before. Kirby didn't overlook it that time and he sure won't this time."

"I figured I couldn't be much worse off, as far as Kirby's concerned," I said. "But it wasn't that. I plain lost my temper. I'd been talking to Allen and I was sore at him. It was like talking to a jellyfish. When I ran into Kirby, all I could think of was that he had hired Tatum, who might have killed us in the Cove and tried like hell to have me killed the night I stayed in town. He isn't even going to be questioned by Allen. You can bet on it. It was just too damn much. I thought he'd go for his gun, but he didn't."

"I didn't think you were an expert with a gun," he said.

"I shoot accurately enough," I said, "but I'm not a fast-draw man. He probably would have killed me, but I wasn't in a frame of mind right then to think about that."

"It's done now," he said. "Maybe you're right. It probably didn't make any difference."

"I pushed him hard enough to make him go for his gun." I said, "but he didn't. You think it means anything?"

"Yeah, it means he's got big enough and rich enough to hire his killings done," Chip said. "So when it came time for him

130

to do it himself, he just wasn't geared up to it. He was a hell of a fast draw years ago, or so I've heard, but I don't think he's been in a gunfight for twenty years. Now, what were you fixing to tell me? When you rode into the stable, you said..."

"I remember," I said, and told him about Tatum, Morck, and Rusk, then added, "There's something else you may not believe. From what you told me, and from the way Janey treated me until a day or so ago, I thought she was the best-natured and sweetest woman who ever drew a breath. She made it plain she liked me. She even came up to my room one night and tried to seduce me. I don't know how I held out, but I got a little scared of the consequences. Anyhow, the truth is she's a bitch."

Chip didn't say anything for a while. he just stared straight ahead, his expression that of a poker player who was plainly trying to hide his feelings. Finally he said, "Explain that. What did she do?"

I told him about the trouble between Susie and Janey, and the two saddlebags and their contents, then I said, "She hasn't really had much love for me since then. Susie says she considered me a ticket out of the Cove. I guess after she knew about the money, she figured she didn't need me if she got a share of it."

"You said Susie told you I had never seen one of their fights," Chip said. "She's right, but I knew they had them, and I knew Janey was resentful as hell about the way their Pa favored Susie. She had a place as long as their mother was alive, but after Mrs. Bowman died, she was a sort of slave girl, or thought she was." He turned his head and looked at me defiantly. "But I honestly thought she would be just right for you. She'd have been so happy getting out of the Cove that she'd have done anything for you."

"Maybe so," I said, not believing it. "The truth is that after you stay on the Rafter B and get to be one of the family, you find out that Susie is one hell of a woman."

"I knew you'd think that," he said. "One reason I wanted you to fall in love with Janey was that I was jealous. I was afraid that Susie would decide you were the man she'd been looking for. I knew she'd never find one she wanted among the bums and idiots and outlaws who lived in the Cove. Ash Morck was the exception. She might have married him, except that he told her plain enough that he wouldn't marry any woman. He was satisfied to sleep with her when he had a chance, and she liked that."

He glanced at me as if he knew damn well that Susie and I had got together, but I didn't tell him how it happened. I said, "I've been curious about this business of you having to go to Hicks to see this man, whoever he is. Do you know him?"

"I've met him several times," Chip said. "I take care of his horse when he's in Canby. We've talked enough for him to know that I wasn't going to shovel horse manure all my life. He wrote me several months ago and said that if I wanted a ranch job, to let him know. I wrote a few weeks ago, and he wrote back to tell me to meet him in Hicks and we'd settle everything. The job is a sort of straw-boss thing. He said we'd better discuss it personally, and he wants me to ride out to his spread and meet the men I'd be working with before I agree to take the job."

I shook my head. "It's got a bad smell to it, Chip. I just don't see the necessity of you riding up there to meet him when you still don't know for sure that you've got the job. You could settle it in a letter."

He nodded. "I've had the same notion, but I figgered he had more reason than he'd given me. Anyhow, I've got to go somewhere. I'll just ride on if I don't get this job. I can take care of myself."

"Sure, you can," I said, "but I'd hate like hell to see you get shot for nothing up there. I don't think Wirt's in this scheme, if that's what it is. He wants Susie convicted, and I don't think he'd interfere by removing her best witness, but I figure Kirby would. He wants you dead because you might keep Susie from going to the pen, and he's capable of murder—as we know from our experience with Tatum."

"So Kirby figgers to get me killed by Galt while I'm in Hicks," he said thoughtfully. "It could be that way, and it's the reason I wanted you with me. Galt will know you're a reporter, and he won't want that kind of publicity."

I let it go at that. Chip had thought about it, and if he was willing to risk his hide, it was his business, but I didn't agree with him on one point. My presence in Hicks wouldn't deter Galt from killing him, if this was a trap as I suspected. I was convinced that neither Kirby nor Galt were the least bit worried about the publicity that a Denver newspaper would give them.

We reached Hicks in the middle of the afternoon. I hadn't expected much of a town, but it was even less than I had anticipated. One hotel, a livery stable, a blacksmith shop, a store with a post office in the back, and a few small buildings that housed the offices of a doctor, a dentist, and a lawyer, along with two or three businesses such as the Colorado-Wyoming Land and Cattle Company. In addition there were ten or fifteen small houses scattered haphazardly on both ends of the business block, plus one log cabin set off by itself to the north.

When I asked Chip what it was, he laughed. "The jail. Also Galt's office. A hell of a place, I tell you. No window in the cell. It stinks. Mattresses full of bedbugs. Don't do anything to make Galt toss you in there."

The road, Main Street, cut through town and continued on north toward Rawlins. Chip told me that the state line ran east and west through the middle of town. Galt held a deputy's badge in both Tremont and Carbon counties, and along with being town marshal, he was the only law within twenty miles in any direction.

We reined up in front of the hotel and tied, Chip saying, "Since he's all the law there is, folks walk easy when they're with him. He's killed at least three men that I've heard of in the last year. He says they were resisting arrest. I call it murder."

We stepped into the hotel lobby. It was empty except for an ancient, tobacco-chewing old man who looked us over, then turned the register for us to sign.

"Go ahead and get a room," Chip said. "I'll wait a while. I may not spend the night here."

I was dead tired. Hungry, too. We hadn't eaten since morning, but what was worse for me was the fact that I hadn't slept much the previous night. I'd spent most of the time in bed on my back, my gun in my hand. I had blocked the hall door, but there was nothing to stop a killer from putting a ladder to the window and crawling into the room. There was no lock on the window and no screen, so I lay there listening for sounds that weren't normal for nighttime. But nothing happened, and now I was in Hicks, so completely worn out that my senses were dulled.

I signed and paid for my room, then joined Chip who had gone into the dining room. I felt better after I had a meal under my belt. I sat back in my chair, my cup of coffee in my hand, and asked, "You supposed to meet your man here?"

He nodded. "Or in the saloon."

We returned to the lobby, paid for our dinners, then Chip asked the clerk, "You seen Arly Tipton today?"

The clerk shook his head. "I ain't seen Arly for a coon's

age. He don't come to town very often."

Chip turned to me. "I'll buy you a drink."

"I'm going to take a nap," I said. "I'll go to sleep standing up if I don't."

"I'll take the horses to the stable," he said. "Go ahead and take your nap. I'll wait in the saloon for Arly."

"Stay out of trouble," I said, "and wake me up if you need me."

He nodded. "Sure," he said, and left the hotel.

I asked for my key and the clerk tossed it onto the counter, saying, "First room to your right at the head of the stairs."

As I climbed the stairs, the terrifying thought came to me that Chip had ridden up here to commit suicide. I tried to put the thought out of my mind, knowing that Chip was too solid a man to do anything that crazy, but I had a hunch that Arly Tipton wasn't going to show up. For a moment I wondered if I should turn around and join Chip in the saloon, but then I remembered what he'd said on the way up here; Chip knew the situation. He was a big boy and he didn't need my nursemaiding. I went on into my room and was asleep the second my head hit the pillow.

Chapter XXIV

I don't know what woke me. For a moment I didn't know where I was, then I remembered my hunch that Arly Tipton wasn't going to keep his date with Chip. The instant I remembered that, a feeling of disaster struck me so forcibly that I was off the bed and buckling my gun belt around me before I was even conscious of what I was doing.

Pouring water into the basin, I sloshed it over my face. I was still groggy from sleep, but the combination of the water and the haunting sense that something tragic was about to happen drove me out of the room and down the stairs. I reached the lobby, then paused to draw my gun and check it, the uneasiness in me growing. I hadn't had many hunches like this, but when I did, I paid attention to them.

I ran into the street, my gun riding loosely in the holster. As I raced along the street to the saloon, the scary thought came to me that I was the one committing suicide by sticking my nose into a row between Chip and Galt. Logic told me to stay out of it, that Galt was a killer, but as I jammed the bat wings apart and stepped into the saloon, I knew very well that logic would not guide my actions.

Chip had a bottle in his hand. He stood facing me, but I'm sure he didn't see me. His gaze was on the man in front of him. This was the first time I'd seen Al Galt; big and broad-shouldered, with a huge head atop a massive neck and a black, drooping mustache that gave him a formidable appearance. He seemed a powerful, overbearing man. He was, I thought, exactly the kind of man I had expected to see, from what I'd heard about him.

Galt wasn't saying anything. He just stood there like a statue in front of Chip, who by now was quite drunk. I had never seen him like that before. He kept waving the bottle around as he shouted, "Your mother was a sheep dog, Galt, a Goddamned sheep dog they never allowed in town. Now why don't you get to hell out of here and let me drink in peace?"

"We don't allow drunks to run loose in town, Malone," Galt said. "You're under arrest. Drop your gun belt and move back."

The half dozen men who were in the saloon had moved back so they wouldn't be in the line of fire. They were motionless, tense, waiting for what to them was inevitable, but I wasn't sure what was going to happen. If Chip went peaceably, and I had a hunch he would, there would be no trouble. If he resisted, Galt would kill him. I didn't want to interfere unless I had to, and afterwards I blamed myself for waiting a few seconds too long.

Chip grinned, the slack-lipped grin of a drunk. He said, "I don't like your Goddamned jail, Galt. You had me in it once, and I told myself I was never going back into it, but I guess I can stand it one night."

It was going to be all right, I told myself. Chip laid the bottle on the bar and lowered his hands to the buckle of his gun belt, and that was when Galt drew his gun, very fast and smooth. Just as Chip's fingers closed on the buckle, Galt shot him.

I was stunned; I couldn't believe I saw what I was seeing. Chip obviously was going to drop his gun belt, to do what Galt had ordered him to, so I had no reason to think Galt was going to do anything more than jail him, but the sound of his gun was like a blast of a cannon in the room. I saw the flash of fire, the rising cloud of black gunsmoke, I smelled the acrid odor. And even though I was watching Galt, I knew that Chip was slammed back by the impact of the big slug, and then went down as if every control of his muscles and joints had given way at once.

Galt paced forward, glancing at the men who were lined up along the wall. He said, "You all saw that he was going for his gun. He was resisting arrest. I had to shoot him." He turned his gaze to the bartender. "You saw it, didn't you, Jake?"

The barman nodded, his lips squeezed tightly together. "Sure, Al," he said. "I saw what happened."

Galt had stopped a step away from Chip's body. He dug a toe into Chip's ribs, but there was no movement. "Dead," Galt said with satisfaction, as he holstered his gun. "Fetch that stretcher you've got in the back room, Jake, and get a couple of men to lug him over to Doc's office."

I had been too stunned and shocked by this cold-blooded killing to move or say anything, but in that instant the paralysis gave way to the same crazy fury that had possessed me the day before when I had grabbed Ike Kirby and shaken him. I didn't give a thought to the possible consequences. I simply yanked my gun from my holster as I yelled, "Galt, you murdering son of a bitch."

He wheeled and drew his gun faster than I had ever seen a man draw. I had my gun in my hand, the hammer back, when he turned, but still he got in the first shot. I fired, wondering why I was still alive when he had clearly pulled the trigger before I did. My bullet nailed him in his barrel-like chest just a split second before he got off his second shot, but he was hard-hit and staggering, and the bullet slapped into the wall two feet above my head.

I hit him two more times as he was falling. He had grabbed the bar and tried to hold himself upright, tried to bring the barrel of his Colt level, but every one of my bullets slammed into his great body. His fingers slid off the bar and he sprawled on the floor a few feet from where Chip lay.

If anyone in the crowd had wanted to pick up Galt's fight, I would have been a dead man. I paced toward him, holding my gun so that if he made a move, I could have fired before he had time to lift it.

He was still breathing when I reached him. He stared up at me, surprised that anyone had the guts to shoot at him. He whispered, "Who the hell are you?"

"A friend of the man you just murdered," I said, and stood there waiting for him to die.

He stared back at me, defiant even now. I wondered what thoughts were going through his head, this man who had shot so many others to death and now must know he was dying the same way.

"Did Kirby pay you to kill Malone?" I asked.

His voice was as defiant as his eyes when he said, "Go to hell!"

That was all. I guess another minute passed before a shudder shook his body, then his mouth gaped open as blood bubbled on his lips and his great head turned and his body was still. He was dead. He had been a tougher man than Van Tatum, who had been a bushwhacking murderer. Tatum had talked, but Galt carried the knowledge of whether he had been hired by Kirby to murder Chip to his grave. I would never know, I thought, but there was no doubt in my mind that it had been a trap, a trap baited by Kirby who, as usual, remained behind the scenes.

I turned to the men who were lined up along the wall. I asked, "Galt got any friends here?"

Only then did they seem to start breathing. They all came to me and shook my hand, one of them saying, "I'm Herb Quincy, the storekeeper and mayor. Galt didn't have a friend on this good earth that any of us knew about. We thank you for killing the bastard."

I shook their hands, then motioned to Chip's body. "I'll go get his horse and take him home." I turned to the barkeep. "Did Chip say anything about a Denver reporter being in town?"

He shook his head. "Not that I heard of."

"Had he been drinking very much?" I asked.

He swallowed and shook his head, his gaze on Chip's body. "No. By God, mister, I just don't understand it. Chip's been here more'n once and done some drinking, but I never seen him drunk, and he put down a hell of a lot less today than usual."

"Thanks," I said, and left the saloon.

I was back in a few minutes with both horses. The bartender and Quincy helped me load Chip's body across the saddle, then the bartender asked, "What's this about a reporter?"

"I'm from the *Denver Chronicle*," I said. "Chip wanted me to come with him because he thought Galt might try to kill him, and he figured that my presence would keep the bastard from trying it. But I did a hell of a poor job taking care of him."

"I'll tell you something," the barman said. "I knew Chip purty well. He often stopped here when he was with the other Cove men taking a herd to Rawlins, and again when he was on his way back. He didn't look to nobody else to take care of him." He stared at me questioningly. "I don't savvy, though. If he had asked you to come with him, why didn't he mention it to Galt?" He made a gesture of futility. "Not that it would have made any difference."

"I don't think it would," I said.

I mounted and rode south, leading Chip's horse. I knew I

couldn't get to the Cove before dark, but I didn't want to stay in Hicks and I didn't want to leave Chip's body there. I had an eerie feeling that he wouldn't have wanted me to leave him.

I rode until it was too dark to see where I was going. I didn't know much about the country because I left the road soon after riding out of Hicks and cut southwest across the sage flat. I found an arroyo with steep banks that would keep me out of the wind, stopped and staked out the horses. I laid Chip close to one of the banks, then built a fire and wished I'd bought some grub in Hicks, but I didn't, so I'd have to make do until I reached the Rafter B.

Question after question raced through my mind. Why hadn't Chip told Galt I was in town? Why had he acted drunk when he wasn't? Had he actually meant for Galt to kill him? Had he finally given up on Susie and, unable to face the future without her, decided on this method of dying? I didn't think so. Nothing that he had said to me gave any hint that he was thinking along that line, and I was convinced he wouldn't have done it before Susie's trial if he had reached any such decision.

By pretending to be drunk and carefully obeying Galt's orders, maybe he thought the marshal would jail him and let it go at that. I suspected he never had been convinced that it was Kirby's plan to lure him to Hicks and have him killed.

I knew I would never have the answers. They had all died with Chip. I had lost a friend, a man I had liked very much. That was all I knew for sure.

It was a long time before I went to sleep.

Chapter XXV

I reined up in front of the Rafter B ranch house just before noon. I dismounted, untied Chip's body, and carried him into the house and laid him on the couch. Janey heard me and ran out of the kitchen. She saw Chip and cried out, "My God," and dropped into the nearest chair, then she began to cry.

A minute or so later Susie came into the house through the back door. She called, "Bob? Chip?" She crossed the kitchen as she said, "I saw your horses . . ." She was in the living room by that time and looked at me. I had moved back from the couch to the other side of the room, so she didn't see the body until I nodded at the couch.

Susie's face became ashen. For several seconds she stood as if frozen. I don't think she saw Janey, who was crying softly, her head in her hands. Susie sat down in a rocker, unable to turn her eyes from the body.

After what seemed a long silence, Susie asked, "How did it happen?"

I told them as briefly as I could, ending with, "It's Kirby's doing. I'm sure of that even if I can't prove it. In a way it's my fault that Chip's dead. I should have jumped Galt as soon as I went into the saloon."

"If you had, you'd have been dead," Susie said hoarsely. "Don't talk any more about it being your fault." She wiped a hand across her face as if she still couldn't believe it had really happened, then she said, "Bob, there's a door in the tool shed and a couple of sawhorses. Bring them in. We'll lay his body out on the door."

I left, glad to be out of the house for a little while. It would be like Susie not to cry and very much like Janey to cry, but I had a hunch that Chip's death hit Susie harder than it had Janey. I wondered if it would occur to Susie that if she had agreed to marry him it wouldn't have happened. I hoped she didn't think of that, because no one could blame her for not marrying a man she didn't love.

Still, I knew Susie would feel guilty, just as I felt guilty for not acting differently than I had when I went into the saloon. Guilty or not, Chip was dead, and both of us would go on living. I hoped she would realize that.

After I had brought the door and the sawhorses into the living room, we moved the body to the door. Susie said, "Ride to the store and tell old-man Frisbee what happened. He'll let everybody know. Folks will want to come this afternoon and pay their respects. Tell Frisbee we'll have the funeral in the morning at eleven. It will be cooler then than in the afternoon."

"I'll tell him," I said.

I turned Chip's horse into the corral, mounted, and rode to the store. Old-man Frisbee shook his head as if all the recent events were too fantastic to have really happened. He said, "I misjudged you, son. I thought you were a lazy, city greenhorn who had come here to sponge off the Bowman girls, but it appears I was wrong."

He held out his hand and I shook it. "Susie said we'd have the funeral at eleven tomorrow and that you'd let folks know," I said.

"I'll take care of everything," he said, "though we'll be digging the grave by lantern light." As I turned to the door, he asked, "Norberg, where is it going to end? Is there anybody who can stop Kirby? Will he murder Susie next?"

"He'll try," I said, and left the store.

I thought about what he had said on my way back to the Rafter B. I wondered if I could get Susie to leave the Cove, to sell out as Janey wanted to do. I didn't think so. The Rafter B had been too much of her life, but I would try.

Frisbee's question had occurred to me before he'd put it into words. Kirby was a madman, so intent on converting the Cove into his winter range that he would continue to murder people until he had removed everyone who would fight. I had a notion that Susie was the only one left.

By the time I got back to the Rafter B, Susie and Janey

had undressed Chip's body. As I went into the house, they were putting a store suit on him. Susie explained that Chip had left the suit here when he'd gone to work in Canby, and had never taken it with him when he'd visited here.

"He didn't have any use for it," Susie told me. "He said we could dress him up for his funeral. I guess he always knew he'd be buried here."

People began coming within the hour, some just to express their sympathy to Susie and Janey and to view the body, and others to help out if they could. Those who came late in the afternoon brought food. I stayed out of the house and cut wood or worked on harness in the barn, or just sat on a sack of grain beside the open door and watched the people come and go.

I was hungry, and wondered if people ate when there was a death in the family. If not, why did the neighbors bring food? Susie came out to the barn near dusk and said a couple of the neighbors had supper ready. We went back into the house holding hands. I don't know which of us reached for the other. All I know is that halfway to the kitchen door I realized we were holding hands.

I'd had time to do a lot of thinking. My job here was done. I'd go back to Canby after the funeral tomorrow and catch the night train to Denver. The odd thing about my feelings was the fact that I didn't want to go. I don't know why I felt that way. I certainly had no intentions of quitting my job with the *Chronicle*. I also had no intention of spending the rest of my life as a ranch hand. I'd had enough of that as a kid, and although I had enjoyed going home and working during my summer vacations, I was always ready to return to Denver when the vacation was over.

If Chip hadn't been killed, I don't think I would have felt this way. Even though he had gone to Hicks hoping to get a job, he was still close enough for either Susie or Janey to reach him in any kind of emergency. Now they had no one except their neighbors, and although they were decent people, I hadn't seen any of them who had impressed me except old-man Frisbee. When he was gone, and that wouldn't be long, the community would simply disintegrate. If Susie went to prison, and I considered the chances good that she would, then there would be nothing to keep Kirby from moving in.

Susie was tough-minded and independent as hell, but she needed somebody, and I think she was realizing it for the first time. I glanced at her in the twilight as we walked to the house and I saw a different Susie than the one I had worked with most of the summer. When we went into the kitchen and sat down at the table with Janey, while a neighbor woman waited on us, I had a strange stirring I had never experienced before, a feeling I could not identify.

Janey ate with her head down. It was evident she had been crying. If Susie had cried, I had not seen any evidence of it, but she was tense, holding herself in a disciplined self-control that made me marvel. I knew she loved Chip as a brother, I knew they had slept together many times in which he had been a lover and not a brother, but I had never been sure just what her feelings were toward him. Either way, she was hard-hit by grief—more than Janey, I thought, and when the dam broke, the tears would come in a torrent.

As soon as we finished eating, the neighbor woman said, "Now you girls go to bed and rest. Mrs. Torrance is staying here tonight. I'll be here, too. No need for either one of you to sit up with the body."

Several people were in the living room. I could hear the low hum of their voices. When I finished eating, I rose and walked toward the back door. Janey remained seated, but Susie rose and followed me. When we were outside, she said, "They all mean well, but after a while I get tired of their sympathy. I'd rather just be with you."

We walked toward the river. I didn't suggest we go there and neither did Susie. We turned that way automatically, neither speaking until we reached the sandy beach and sat down near the edge of the water. I think in this time of grief we both wanted to share the spiritual peace that comes from flowing water, a sense of God's presence. I was not a deeply religious man, and I had never heard Susie mention the subject, but I am convinced that at a time of emotional distress, people instinctively seek comfort from a Divine Presence, even though they may not be church-goers.

We sat in silence for a long time, with the stars and a sickle of a moon shining from a cloudless sky. I heard no sound except the rustle of the water and a coyote bark from the rim of the cliff on the other side of the river. Later an owl's hoot came from somewhere upstream.

Then I heard Susie begin to cry, and suddenly the dam broke as I knew it would and she was weeping, her whole body shaken by her sobs. I slipped an arm around her, and she put her head on my shoulders and cried for a long time. I felt like crying, too, but the tears wouldn't come.

After a while the sobs were not so loud and didn't wrench her body as they had been, then there was only a series of low moans, and after that silence. Presently she put an arm around me and held me with a fierce grip as if she would never let me go.

"I don't know what I would have done without you, Bob," she said in a low tone. "When you first came, I hated you. I didn't want you around. It seemed wrong for you to be sticking your nose into our business, but it's all changed now. I know it was more than our business. Maybe the publicity you'll give us will change things and even keep me out of prison."

"I hope so," I said. "It's the reason I came, but that's changed, too. I hated Kirby before because of what happened to my father, but that was only a whim compared to what I feel about the man now."

"We both feel guilty," she said, "and we shouldn't. You think you could have prevented Chip's death if you had known what was going to happen..."

"Or if I had gone into the saloon with him instead of taking a nap," I said.

"And I know that if I had married him," she said, "he wouldn't have gone to Hicks. My feelings for Chip were always mixed up. I thought of him as a brother, but when he came back after being gone for a while, I slept with him because he wanted to and I needed a man. The trouble was, I soon began feeling that it was wrong, that we were committing incest. I have never been one to worry about sin and morals, but I did think about that, so I would send him upstairs after a few days. That's why I knew I couldn't marry him."

"Then you have no business feeling guilty," I said.

"I know," she said. "Neither do you."

"I guess so," I said, but it was going to take more than her words to erase my guilty feelings.

"What are you going to do now," she asked.

"I'll stay till after the funeral," I said, "then I'm going back to Denver and see if I still have a job."

"I don't know what I'll do without you," she said. "Janey will be gone. I may even go to prison."

"I'm coming back for the trial," I said. "Maybe I can help."

"I know you can." She rose and, reaching down, took my hands and pulled me to my feet. She stood facing me, her arms still around me, her head tipped back to stare at me in the darkness. She added, "The hell of it is that Ike Kirby is still alive and will go unpunished."

I pulled her to me and kissed her, feeling very tender and loving at that moment toward her, with the knowledge in me that behind the facade of strength and toughness was a fine and beautiful woman who would strip that facade away if given the right opportunity.

We walked back to the house, slowly, as if not wanting to lose this beautiful, warm feeling we shared. Then what she had just said about Kirby got through to me, and I realized that my business in Tremont County was not finished.

Chapter XXVI

Chip's funeral was different from Morck's and Rusk's. It was held in the same place, the people were the same, but somehow it was different. Old-man Frisbee said almost the same words, except that he added several minutes to talk about Chip's life in the Cove—how he had been raised by Alec Bowman as a son and as Susie and Janey's brother, and the fat woman played and sang the same hymns, but the difference was deeper than anything so superficial.

It is hard to explain something which is beneath the surface and therefore not visible, or even tangible, but it had to do with the intensity of emotion. The Cove people had liked Morck and Rusk and had accepted them, but they had been outsiders. Chip was one of them, and I honestly think that every family in the Cove felt as if a son had been lost.

All the women except Susie were crying. She sat in a front seat, her face stony-hard. The men, too, were dabbing at their eyes. Several broke down, especially when the coffin was being lowered and the grave filled. I was close to breaking down myself, so I turned and walked away and stood beside the buggy while Susie and Janey were being hugged and kissed by the women. The word had spread that I had shot and killed Al Galt, who was well known by reputation in the Cove. I think every man there shook my hand before I drove away, with Susie beside me in the front seat and Janey in the back.

I stopped in front of the Rafter B ranch house and both women got out. I drove to the barn, unhooked, watered the horses, and stripped the harness from them. I started toward the kitchen door, but before I reached it Susie came rushing out of the house and passed me without even glancing at me, her face as stony-hard as it had been at the funeral.

I turned and stared at her back, then noticed she was wearing a gun, and I remembered what she had said the night before about Ike Kirby being alive and going unpunished. I ran after her and stepped in front of her and made her stop.

"Now just hold on a Goddamned minute," I said, gripping her shoulders. "I've got a stake in this, too. I'm going with you."

"No, you're not," she flared. "Chip was a Bowman. That makes it my business. If my father was alive, he'd attend to this, but he isn't, so it's up to me."

I was mad then. "You're still playing the role of a man. I thought you'd finally accepted the fact that you are a woman, and you were going to start acting like one."

Her expression didn't change. "Tell me that tomorrow. That's when I start being a woman."

"No, I'm telling you today," I said. "I know how Chip would have felt about this. I can't stop you, but I can go with you. Maybe I can't save your life any more than I saved Chip's, but at least I've got the right to go with you."

"Get out of my way, Bob," she said ominously. "I love you, but I'll knock your teeth out if you don't move."

So she loved me! I was shocked, never expecting to hear those words from Susan Bowman. I stared at her angry, rebellious face, not sure how she could say that and still look and feel the way she did. I did the first thing that came into my mind. I already had my hands on her shoulders. I put my arms around her and brought her to me and kissed her. I shall never forget that kiss as long as I live. It was long, it was passionate, and it told me a great deal about Susie Bowman I had not known before. The stiffness went out of her and she clung to me, crying softly.

"I've wanted you to do that for a long time," she said. "I guess you're the first man I ever met that I knew I could marry. I know it wouldn't work out, with you loving your job the way you do and me being a lousy cook and housekeeper, but you've shown me qualities in a man that I did not know existed."

"We've got a lot to talk about when we get back," I said. "Wait till I get my gun."

I ran into the kitchen. Janey was standing motionless in the middle of the room. I hurried past her and went upstairs. I buckled my gun belt around me and raced back down the stairs and past Janey who hadn't moved.

"Where are you and Susie going?" she demanded.

I paused by the back door. "Susie didn't say?"

Janey shook her head. "She just said she'd be back later this afternoon."

"We're paying Ike Kirby a visit," I said.

I left the house on the run and went on out to the corral where Susie had just saddled her horse. I saddled Prince and caught up with Susie, who had gone on to the road and turned toward the steep slope that led out of the Cove.

Neither of us said a word for a long time. I guess we didn't want to tackle the thorny problem of our future. I'm sure Susie wasn't thinking past the encounter with Kirby, and I found myself caught in a bog of cross-currents and regrets.

Susie had done nothing to make me like her when I had first come to the Rafter B. I had turned to Janey, who had seemed to have all the qualities I admired in a woman. It had been extremely painful to discover that she was not the woman I had thought she was, that I had not met the real Jane Bowman until she had seen the saddlebags and the money they contained.

I suppose that my attitude about women being cheats and deceivers went back to my early twenties, and experiences that had been difficult to forget. I had tried not to think of them, but I knew now that Janey's turnaround had brought back all the old misery I had tried to forget. I thought I had succeeded.

Now Susie, who pretended to be as tough as a cob but was honest and straightforward, had told me in her forthright way that she loved me. It was a strange moment to be thinking about women and love and the future, but the thoughts were there. It was going to take time to sort them out.

Susie reined up when we reached the forks in the road, one leading to Canby, the other to Hatchet. I pulled in beside her, asking, "Got a hunch about which way to go?"

"No," she answered. "Have you?"

"He might be in Utah now," I said, "but he had some horses coming in from Wyoming and he was to be out here to look at them when they arrived, so if they haven't got here yet, he'll be at Hatchet."

"Then we'll go there," she said.

"And if he's in Utah?"

She gave me a tight-lipped grin. "We'll go to Utah."

We rode slowly, scanning the horizon. If his hands were here, we were riding into a hornet's nest. I didn't know how Susie felt about that. Her life had been so screwed up lately that it was possible she didn't care whether she lived or died, but I knew I wasn't ready to die. If the odds were too great against us, I was all for going back to the Cove but, knowing Susie as well as I did, I didn't say it.

We reached Hatchet without seeing anyone. Only a single horse was in the corral next to the barn. Maybe it meant something, that Kirby was here alone and within our reach. We reined in behind the barn and dismounted, leaving our horses here so they wouldn't be seen from the house.

"You want to go on with this?" I asked.

She looked at me as if it was a stupid question, and again, knowing Susie as well as I did, I guess it was. She said, "Of course. Come on."

She started across the dust-covered yard between the house and the barn, walking fast, her head turning from one side to the other as if expecting someone to pop out of the house or one of the outbuildings. We had, as the saying went, crossed the Rubicon. There was no turning back. No planning, no discussion of how we were going to do this. We'd bull straight ahead and hope. That was my Susie. I couldn't turn around and leave the job up to her, so I strode beside her, expecting a bullet from the house any minute.

We reached the porch and eased across it to the front door that was wide open. Still there was no sound from inside the house, no hint that anyone was there. I stood motionless on one side of the door, my gun in my hand. Susie had moved to the other side. She looked at me questioningly as she drew her gun and cocked it. Neither of us knew what to do next. I still couldn't believe that we had crossed the yard between the house and the barn without being seen. We were, I decided, walking into a trap, but there wasn't anything else to do.

If Kirby was here and had seen us, why hadn't he smoked us down before we reached the house? Maybe he wasn't in the house, but I had a hunch he was. I didn't question my hunches when they were as strong as this, so I had to go on the assumption that he was in the house.

I didn't know why he hadn't gunned us down as we crossed the yard, unless it was the same reason that he hadn't drawn on me that afternoon in the courthouse. The habit of passing on his unpleasant chores to men like Van Tatum and Al Galt was so strong that he had trouble facing them himself. For a crazy moment I almost laughed. Unless someone else was in the house, this was one time Ike Kirby was on his own.

I edged forward so I could see into the living room. It was empty, as I was sure it would be, a room almost devoid of furniture. There was an open door on the far side of the room that led into the kitchen. I could hear someone back there rattling pans. So Kirby wasn't alone. If it was the cook, I figured there was a chance he'd stay out of it.

Sweat was breaking out all over me. I wiped my face, glanced at Susie, and jerked my head toward the room to indicate I was going in. Susie nodded. I slipped through the door and put my back to the wall and Susie came in and moved to the opposite side of the door.

Now I discovered there was another door on my left. It probably opened into a bedroom, or maybe an office. Kirby was in that room. I was as sure as if I could see him. If I yanked the door open and rushed into that room, he'd cut me down. The chances were he was standing there waiting for us, a gun in his hand.

If it was a trap, so be it. I had to root him out, so I slowly angled toward the door, every nerve on edge. I was halfway across the room when the door slammed open and Kirby lunged out, his gun smoking. He was fanning his gun, the first time I had ever seen a man do it, a trick he had probably learned when he was in the habit of using his gun.

He got off three shots before I could pull the trigger. I had not expected him to make a move like this, so I was startled and a second slow. Susie beat me to it. Her first bullet caught Kirby in the chest. He was slammed back and was falling by the time my first slug hit him.

Susie didn't move. She had fired only once, but it had been enough, a perfect shot that must have blown his heart to pieces. He was dead by the time I knelt beside him. I rose and for a moment stood looking down at him—a small man who had been guilty of more evil than any other man I had ever met, but now one bullet had cut his malevolent power from him. If it had happened sooner, Chip Malone would still be alive.

When I turned, the cook had come out of the kitchen. He stood just inside the living room, his hands in the air. He was an old man, skinny, with a face scarred by wrinkles. Probably he had been a cowboy in his youthful days until, bunged up by rheumatism and age, he had turned to cooking.

"I ain't in this," the old man cried shrilly. "I've got no reason to pick up that bastard's fight."

"You see him start the shooting?" I asked.

"I seen him and I'll tell the sheriff if he asks me," the cook said. "I always got along fine when he stayed in town or was in Utah or Wyoming, but when he was here, I couldn't do nothing right." He stared at the dead man, his lips curled in distaste. "He was a genuwine son of a bitch."

I holstered my gun and turned to the door. The old man called, "One thing, mister. You'd better move out fast. His crew is fetching in a band of horses, and they'll be along any time. They'll pick up his fight if they catch you."

We crossed the yard, Susie holding a hand to her side, but I didn't know she'd been hit until we got around the barn and I had started to mount. She collapsed ten feet from her horse, saying, "I can't make it, Bob. He nailed me where it hurts."

I knelt beside her, unable to believe what had happened. I thought all of Kirby's shots had gone wild, but his last one must have been the slug that did the damage. She had been hit in the belly and now her life was spilling out of her in a scarlet flood.

She lifted a hand and felt of my face. "I'm glad I had a chance to know you, Bob. If this hadn't happened, I'd have done my best to get you to marry me. I'd even learn to cook." She tried to smile, then whispered. "Kiss me one more time, Bob."

I kissed her, one arm supporting her, then she pushed me away, saying softly, "Good riding, Bob, all the way."

She died then, and all I could do was to let her head sink to the ground and sit there and stare at her. I was paralyzed, and then I began to cry, the first time since I'd been a boy. There had been plenty of times when I had wanted to cry. Now the tears came and I thought they would never stop.

The tears were still running down my cheeks when I rose and lifted her into the saddle and lashed her body into place. I wondered how many more times I would have to do this before I got out of Tremont County. Or if anybody would do this for me if Kirby's crew caught up with me. I told myself I'd make it. With any luck, I'd be out of the country in a few hours.

When I got back to the Rafter B, another shock waited for me. I carried Susie's body into the house and laid it on the door that had held Chip's body. I looked at her face, pale, lifeless, not

151

at all resembling the face of the Susan Bowman I had known.

"Janey," I yelled.

No answer. I went into the kitchen. A note was on the table. I picked it up and read: "I, Jane Bowman, being of sound mind and knowing exactly what I am doing, leave my half share of the Rafter B to my sister, Susan Bowman, to sell or do with as she pleases. *Jane Bowman*."

I stared at the note, not comprehending the full significance of it for a moment. I only knew it was not like Janey to do this. They had to be an explanation. Then I thought of the money. Morck's and Rusk's saddlebags! I ran into Susie's bedroom. The saddlebags had been tossed into a corner. I picked them up. There were, as I had known they would be, empty.

I thought: *Now Janey has the means to see the big world that's out there*.

I walked out of the house, carrying Susie's body, and tied it across the saddle again. I rode to the store and told old-man Frisbee what had happened.

He stared across the valley to the hills that rimmed it on the north, the corners of his mouth working. He swallowed, then managed to say, "I knew it was going to happen some way. She done what she had to do. It was like her." He swiped a hand across his eyes, then turned his gaze to me. "I don't want to see you no more. Every time you ride in here, you're fetching another body."

"I don't aim to see you any more," I said. "I'm headed for Canby and aim to catch the night train to Denver, but there's chores to do on the Rafter B, a cow to milk and chickens to feed and..."

"They'll be done," he said.

I turned and mounted Prince. I didn't know what would happen to the Rafter B, but it wasn't my job to stay there and find out. My job would be finished when I got to Denver and wrote up the end of the story I had come here to write. Susan Bowman would never be tried for rustling.

When I rode past the Rafter B ranch house, I had a lump in my throat I couldn't swallow. The time I had spent here had been both sweet and bitter, dull and exciting, loving and hating, and ending in a different way than it had started.

I put Prince up the steep slope, following the road that led out of the Cove, and headed out across the sage flat, thinking that Sid Gorman would have his story. It wouldn't be what I had expected to write, or what Sid had expected, but it was still one hell of a story

And Susie? One thing was sure. I would cherish the memory of her as long as I lived. Like the story about her, she had been one hell of a woman.

"REACH FOR THE SKY!"

and you still won't find more excitement or more thrills than you get in Bantam's slam-bang, action-packed westerns! Here's a roundup of fast-reading stories by some of America's greatest western writers: